DEADSTICK
Terence Faherty

W⊕RLDWIDE.

TORONTO • NEW YORK • LONDON
AMSTERDAM • PARIS • SYDNEY • HAMBURG
STOCKHOLM • ATHENS • TOKYO • MILAN
MADRID • WARSAW • BUDAPEST • AUCKLAND

For Jan

DEADSTICK

A Worldwide Mystery/May 1995

First published by St. Martin's Press, Incorporated.

ISBN 0-373-26167-5

Printed in U.S.A.

★

"It doesn't make sense," I said. "Why reopen the investigation at all if they're afraid of finding something?"

"I've been thinking, Owen. Maybe you're right. Maybe Bonsett's orders aren't coming from Carteret. After all, the legal department reports to Carolyn Vernia." Harry didn't really mind my playing Paul Drake, as long as I let him be Perry Mason.

"Why would she even be interested?"

"Carl Vernia." His good humor was returning with enthusiasm. "He's the only one who profited from William's death. Carolyn may know that her father could be implicated."

★

"...Faherty displays an assured talent for plot and character."

—*Publishers Weekly*

"A sure-handed debut..."

—*Kirkus Reviews*

"Faherty shows himself to be a good observer of human nature."

—*Courier Times* (PA)

DEADSTICK

PREHISTORY

I STILL HAVE the dream some nights. It is always 1941, a time before I was born. October 10, 1941, although I'm not aware of the date while I'm dreaming. In the dream, I'm walking along in the country. In a field. It's a sunny day. I can see my solitary shadow preceding me across the tall grass and wild flowers, the shadow an elongated version of myself, boyish looking and gangly. I'm at peace at that moment, but it's a thoughtless, uncaring peace. The field is full of a gentle buzzing, and it fills my head, but it may also be that the buzzing from my head is spreading out over the field.

Gradually, I become aware of a different sound, a droning that at first forms a harmony with the bright blue buzzing of the field. Slowly, the droning grows and grows, not so much overlaying the buzzing as shouldering it sideways out of my head. Then I look up and see the plane. It's a tiny thing, so close to the midday sun that I hold my hand up as a shield and squint to see it. The plane is black against the brightness. I note the large round engine that dwarfs the plane behind it, the engine whose droning sound has silenced my field. I wonder about the lucky people who are riding in the plane thousands of feet above me. I feel a moment's envy of them, wondering who they are. I am wondering, too, where they are coming from and where they are going and envying them their destination without knowing what it is.

I have the odd idea then that my questions are supporting the plane somehow, just as its short, rounded wings support it in the bright sky. By wondering about it and by being here, alone in this field, to see it pass, I am confirming its existence, sustaining its reality. I have the feeling that without me or some other person to hear the droning engine, without some sympathetic soul to wonder about the privileged passengers and to worry about their danger, the plane would cease to exist. Or worse, it would fall from the sky like a stone.

As I have that thought, as the plane passes directly above me, its droning motor stops. It is replaced, not by the warm, lazy buzzing, but by a silence more frightening than crashing thunder. I feel my heart begin to race and my breath grow short while I stand, staring upward. Did some unspoken doubt of mine cause the engine to stop? I note a gentle rocking of the plane's wings, and then it noses over and falls toward me. It spins like a dead leaf falling from a tree, slowly at first and then faster and faster, the huge engine a pivot around which the helpless plane races. All at once, the spinning stops and my heart swells with silent cheer. The pilot is in control again, I think, he will save the plane. I wave my arms frantically, trying to draw the pilot's attention to my broad field, but the plane—gliding down silently toward the ground—flies away from me.

I begin to run after the plane, afraid of losing sight of it, desperate not to fail the people inside it. As I run, I realize that my sunlit field has become a dark forest. I run a drunken line through the trees, branches and brush pulling at my clothes. For a time, I can still see the plane through the treetops. It has grown enormously, and its black shape fills half the sky. Then it is too low for me to see. I strain through the awful silence to hear the sound of the plane striking the trees. Instead I hear, faintly, the sound of a man laughing a dry cackling laugh. Then I hear a murmur of voices that slowly rises, men's and women's voices speaking at once, the words jumbled together in a hopeless tangle like the forest before me.

My one thought is to find the plane, and I repeat the goal over and over to myself to block out the jumbled messages: Find it, find it, find it.

Then, my progress all but stopped by the grasping branches, I hear a single voice rise above the others. It is a voice I know but cannot place, a soft, sad voice that says: "You never will."

ONE

It was October 1981. I was in Harry's office to hear about an old case or a new case, I didn't know which. I should drop the pretense of calling them cases right away. Harry never liked that little joke of mine. They were not cases, they were only odd jobs, and I was not a detective, I was only a researcher. A legal aide with a library card, as Harry once put it. Though I was not a detective, some days as I worked I felt a déjà vu that came, I realized, not from some memory of my own past but from a half-remembered page of a paperback book. In that kind of book, a detective tells his own story because he is his only witness and confidant. That was my situation in those days, so I will follow the pattern and tell you my story myself. I can tell it now because time has passed and people have died. One person in particular. My name, incidentally, is Owen Keane.

In 1981 Harry was in the process of assuming control of Ohlman, Ohlman, and Pulsifer, Attorneys at Law, a firm his father had founded. Harold Ohlman, Sr., might have been just another name in the family's Boston firm, but for the shingle being full. He became instead the first name of a New York City branch. Harry's was the second name, of course. I very seldom saw Mr. Pulsifer, but I had a sympathetic feeling for him. Another Ohlman appearing from anywhere could have knocked him as far south as Philadelphia. Mr. Ohlman's genteel Boston background accounted for the general air of our firm, which was staid and respectable. The law being a common profession, the successful firm will be the one with the specialty. Respectability or, rather, discretion was our stock in trade, the proper, well mannered, gentlemanly approach to the improper. We cleaned up other people's messes and kept pleasant people out of unpleasant contexts. I would be pretending again, however, if I claimed to know how Ohlman, Ohlman, and Pulsifer had really worked during my tenure. I never gave it that much of my attention.

Inattention had been a growing problem for me in the years after college. I had failed to reach my only concrete goal, the priesthood, and that failure had set the pattern for my next few years. After leaving the seminary, I had spiraled down through a series of less challenging jobs. Then Harry had reached out and rescued me by creating a position for me with his firm. The job Harry came up with didn't help my wandering mind. In fact, it seemed designed around my limited attention span. My duties were restricted to library research, except for a rare field trip thrown in for variety. My research subjects were generally circumscribed and my deadlines were kept carefully short. The condescension behind this design didn't bother me. I considered the position not so much a job as a way of acting out my days. At least I did until this particular October morning.

I sat quietly in a comfortable chair whose upholstery made my suit seem cheap and unsubstantial. Harry sat across an impressive expanse of polished walnut, signing his name. His secretary, Ms. Kiefner, stood silently at his elbow, her yellow dress reflected in the wood. Ms. Kiefner was a humorless lady of about forty whose behavior toward me always suggested that her name could pop up on the stationery after Mr. Pulsifer's at any moment. The decor of Harry's office was cold and impersonal, except for one of Harry's own oil paintings that was all but hidden between massive bookcases, and the atmosphere always dampened what remained of our old camaraderie. I never felt odd about working for Harry when I considered it as an abstraction over breakfast. But in the office, Harry's office, this old college friend seemed to be someone else entirely, and I felt slightly compromised. In school I'd gotten into the habit of seeing myself in Harry, by defining Harry and noting the differences between us, and it had been a satisfying process. Recently, I'd come to find the old practice less comfortable.

It had never bothered me that Harry was more impressive physically, bigger and better looking. In the last category, he'd actually lost a little ground in the ten years since we'd graduated from Boston College. His suits were well made, but their cut was becoming cosmetic. His dark hair was thinning prematurely, forcing his part lower, it seemed, every time I saw him. The change that bothered me was subtler than any physical plus or minus. Harry had acquired a spiritual advantage over me. He had successfully worked out questions that he'd probably never asked himself. It was the sense of who he was and what he was doing with his life that had changed him right down to the way he now signed his name.

Ms. Kiefner gathered the signed papers and left, pausing a moment to place a single sheet facedown on my side of the desk. Harry and his secretary's unspoken communication made me feel even less comfortable.

"I want you to know I've enjoyed the work you've done on the Omax divestiture," Harry began. "Climax, Colorado, in the gold rush days. Great reading. Twenty-five typed pages and you haven't even gotten to the twentieth century."

"There's a lot of material," I said.

"None that pertains to our client's suit, apparently. Never mind. I'll have someone else finish up on that. I have a new subject for you, one that you'll like. There's no point to it, and the more volume you produce the better." Harry seemed to remember something. He shook his head and smiled. "Sorry I jumped right into it, Owen. It's been a busy morning. Mary's been asking about you. She wants to know when you're coming out to meet Amanda."

Mary was Harry's wife and Amanda was their new daughter. "How are those two?" I asked.

"Amanda's a doll," Harry said without sounding exactly sure. She was their first. "Mary's good, too. You know Mary."

I nodded. I had known Mary quite well, once upon a time.

"She's already back in her routine," Harry said. "She's involved in so many charities and causes, I can't name them all." His smile became less practiced for a moment. "To tell you the truth, I don't see them all that much myself. Not as much as I should. I complained enough when Dad was here full time, but now I miss him."

"You don't have to go up to the roof now to practice your clarinet," I said.

"I don't even have time to think about the clarinet or painting or anything else. Sometimes I wish I'd gone into a more straightforward law practice. I haven't Dad's talent for coddling eccentricity. But I'm wandering, and I really only have a few minutes."

"I understand," I said.

"We'll crack one of those bottles behind the Blackstone some night and have a real talk, I promise."

"Yes," I said.

"Yes. Anyway, to start again, have you ever heard of Robert Carteret?"

"No."

"Don't feel bad, not many people have. He's the Howard Hughes of Long Island. How about the Carteret Corporation?"

"Carteret Federal Bank?"

"That's the golden goose, but they're into a lot of things now. They own a leasing company, I think, and some sort of data processing operation. Robert Carteret owns the bank and everything it owns."

"And he keeps a low profile."

"He keeps no profile. I'd be willing to bet that even a bloodhound like you couldn't find a photograph of him taken after 1945. I doubt one exists."

"Does he exist?" I asked.

"You see before you a piece of prima facie evidence."

I leaned forward and picked up the sheet of paper Ms. Kiefner had left. It was a photocopy of a typed letter:

Dear Sir:

This is to empower you to investigate the plane

crash that claimed the life of my brother, William Carteret, and his fiancée on October 10, 1941. I require all the details that can be determined with dispatch and discretion.

                                        Robert Carteret

The paper bore no letterhead. Carteret's faint signature would have been indecipherable without the typed name below it.

"It's not addressed to us," I observed.

"No. I received it yesterday with a cover letter from the head of the Carteret Corporation's legal department. He considered it inappropriate for the corporation to handle it."

"Inappropriate?"

"His word, which he didn't bother to explain. I'd suggest that they didn't want Carteret employees rooting around in the Carteret past. Our involvement evidently stems from some work Dad did for them years ago. Dad didn't specifically describe it when I discussed the business with him last night, but he may have forgotten it."

"Did your father have any idea why research on a forty-year-old plane crash would justify such elaborate treatment?"

Harry settled back in his chair, which made him seem quite far away. "For one thing," he said, "the request is over Robert Carteret's signature. I gather that he's considered a kind of mythical beast by the people who work for him. I can imagine the shock waves that letter generated, sort of like Con Ed getting a memo from Menlo Park. He isn't what you'd call an active man. Dad thinks he was wounded during the Second World War. I doubt many of his employees have ever seen him. Are you still smoking?''

I nodded no and watched him light a cigarette. He took an ashtray from a desk drawer, which suggested that he'd quit, too.

''There's another reason why this job may have been too hot for the corporation to handle,'' Harry said. ''It seems there was a scandal connected with the crash. Dad has heard stories about it, of course.''

Of course, I repeated to myself. Like all discreet people, Harold Ohlman, Sr., was a lightning rod for gossip.

Harry drew deeply on his cigarette before continuing. ''A little family history first. William Carteret was Robert's older brother. Their father, Charles Carteret, was the founder of the bank. You could do a great report on him, book length. He'd evidently been involved in New York City politics when the operation still turned a profit. Dad thinks he died a year or so before the accident.''

''Did William inherit?'' I asked, jumping slightly ahead.

''Yes, and he got just about everything. Charles must have wanted his little kingdom to survive intact. We won't go into injustices caused by asinine wills, out of professional courtesy. William received the bank and the family estate on Long Island, which came with an airfield and a plane. Actually, the plane was probably William's all along. He died at the end of an era of playboy aviators. Anyway, he and his fiancée, whose name Dad couldn't recall, took off on a flight one day and disappeared.''

''Where were they heading?''

Harry smiled for no apparent reason. "From the Long Island estate to Albany, where she had family. Most of New York State was searched without result." He paused and smoked his cigarette for a moment's effect. "Nine months later, the wreck of the plane was found in a New Jersey forest, a hundred miles or so south of the Carteret estate. William and the girl were still in it, what was left of them."

"Nine months?" I asked.

"Yes. I guess William's flight plan was pretty casual. There was a lot of speculation at the time the plane disappeared and some national press. You shouldn't have any problem finding some newspaper accounts. Dad thought there might even have been a report that they'd landed in Ireland. Of course, that was all in the fall of '41. After Pearl Harbor two months later it was pretty much forgotten."

"It still seems incredible that the wreck of a plane could go unnoticed for nine months in a state as crowded as New Jersey," I said, thinking aloud. "Maybe that's what's bothering Robert."

"I doubt it. According to Dad, the old rumors were nastier than that. There was a brief inquiry when the wreck was found, but no real explanation for the crash was ever officially announced. However, there may have been some evidence to suggest that someone had tampered with the plane before the flight."

"What sort of evidence?"

"I don't know. I don't know that there really was any. The scandal was old news when Dad first heard of it, remember, but he described it more as a feeling people had. Dad really didn't want to go into that part. Robert stood to gain everything from his brother's death. That was enough to start people talking."

"So Robert inherited from William."

"Eventually. He was in the army overseas when the plane was found."

"Wait a minute," I said. "The plane was found in July of '42? That was only seven months after Pearl Harbor. Robert must have been the first man to enlist."

"He didn't enlist. There was a peacetime draft in 1941. Robert was caught in it. At least that's the story Dad heard. Robert reported for duty shortly after the plane disappeared, which must have put the rumor mill on overtime."

"His corporation didn't have enough pull to exempt him?"

"He wasn't exempted."

"And he was wounded?"

"Yes, decorated, too. I don't know any of the details, except that he seemed to use his medical discharge to excuse himself from the rest of his life. He still lives in the Long Island house, but he's sold a lot of the property. Dad didn't say if he'd ever actually met Robert. I know I haven't, and I can't say I know anyone who has."

"What does he do?"

"Anything he wants to, I suppose. I wasn't kidding before when I compared him to Howard Hughes, except that he beat Hughes to it. I know he sponsors a horse show every year at Great Bay, but I don't think he ever attends. I've seen his name on charity committees and patron lists, but I don't know if he or his accountants are really involved."

"Who minds the store?"

"That's more straightforward, naturally. A man named Carl Vernia ran the bank until his death in 1968. He'd been with the company since the time of Charles Carteret. There were a couple different presidents in the next few years. In 1973, Vernia's daughter, Carolyn, took over. She's been running it ever since."

"Old Dad must have had some pull, or did he leave sealed instructions?"

"Let me remind you that we don't consider nepotism a joking matter in this office."

"Good point," I said. "I won't underestimate Carolyn Vernia."

"Don't worry about it. You'll never come within a mile of her in your social wanderings. And certainly not in connection with this business." Harry ground his cigarette stub in the ashtray and considered it seriously for a moment before lighting a second.

"I know it's your decision, Harry," I said, "but why are we even bothering with this?"

"If I stopped to ask myself that every morning, we'd both starve to death. Small things lead to big things if they're handled well, Owen. This business is half reputation and half connections. Robert Carteret is a valuable connection."

"Just asking."

"I know. I also know how easily your 'whys' can get out of hand."

"Sorry," I said.

"Don't apologize. I'm glad you don't see this business as an excuse to unravel dark mysteries." We smiled together, Harry's last remark having embarrassed us both with its thinly veiled reference to my past preoccupations. "Think of this as one more history paper." Harry said. "Okay?"

"Okay," I said.

"Dad wasn't certain what would please Carteret," Harry said. "Frankly, he wasn't sure anything would."

"You mentioned volume before," I said tactfully.

"I meant your usual thorough treatment. Dad feels it's worth our while to go along with Carteret, or rather it's worth a week or two of your time. There should be some public record of the case that can be reworked into a neatly typed report."

His tone told me that I should stand.

"I'll tell Mary that you were asking about her," he said. "And I was serious about that drink; maybe we can work it in with a progress report."

"Yes," I said.

He ground his cigarette into the ashtray and pushed it across to my side of the desk. "Do me a favor," he said. "As you go by Ms. Kiefner, cough."

For once I left Harry's office feeling happier than I'd been when I'd entered it. I would have taken any assignment in exchange for Omax, but it was more than that. This new case, this forty-year-old accident, forgotten before the victims were buried, intrigued me. Harry had kidded me about playing detective once or twice since I'd come to work for him, but I'd never really had that much to play with. My usual expeditions through the dusty leavings of some stranger's life were always unsatisfying and ultimately empty; they led nowhere but further back into things less meaningful for being so long gone. I sensed from the start that the Carteret case would be different, which turned out to be a rare example of a Keane hunch proving correct. For at the end of this trail of the dead and forgotten I would find something alive and forgotten, whose faint heartbeat grew louder as I wound my way backward.

TWO

I WENT TO WORK on my new job that same day, as soon as I was able to divest myself of Omax. Harry's criticism of my work on that assignment had been well founded. I had made the basic mistake of accumulating more facts than I could possibly interpret. Omax was a large, aggressive mining company that had literally been changing the face of its earth for a hundred years. During that period its corporate pride had been expressed autobiographically in a thousand press releases and pamphlets, dozens of annual reports, and even a memoir or two. Fact on top of fact, none of which or all of which reflecting a basic truth about the company which I simply could not discern. What had they really found in the first spadeful of ore taken and in the mountains since? What did that first Harvard geologist, lost in Colorado, have to do with the multinational that now advertised during the Super Bowl? I never found out. I understood that Harry had been interested in some names and dates. In any case, I left us both unsatisfied.

Now Harry wanted the same superficial level of information, the same yearbook summary, for a forty-year-old plane crash. I had already decided that our mysterious client wanted more. I didn't believe I could add substantially to any list of details on the crash that Robert Carteret could have compiled himself in the years since the war. I didn't believe that Carteret wanted me to. I was already whimsically reinterpreting his letter as my authorization to string those facts together, to find whatever truth there was behind them. To solve the mystery of his brother's last flight. The only problem with this view of things was Robert's reluctance to share the basic pieces of the puzzle. I was forced, therefore, to complete the preliminary research that Harry saw as the whole job.

Our offices were in the Johnson Tyre Building, on Forty-second Street east of Madison. It was a short walk to my mean streets, the New York Public Library. I liked to walk to the library because it gave me the time to plan my day. I'd already set off pages of my notebook with subject headings, in the approved researcher fashion. The categories were biographical: William Carteret, Robert Carteret, Charles Carteret, Carl Vernia; historical: crash—newspaper account, crash—official inquiry; and technical: description of plane, evidence of sabotage. In addition to this written agenda, I was already forming a mental list of more interesting questions. What Harry might have called my "uncontrollable whys."

Why, I silently asked a hairy traffic cop, did Carteret fly south? It might have been a rich man's whim; the trip to Albany might always have been a blind. My razor-sharp researcher instinct told me that it was an important question to answer. I felt that the implication of sabotage would be easier to define if any sort of public record existed of the crash inquiry. Robert's military service also intrigued me, especially the timing of it. Had his rush to defend Great Bay actually been an attempt to escape? And why hadn't his family's money and connections kept him out of the reach of a peacetime draft?

I directed my next question to a lady in a grayed pink housedress. Why would a millionaire in his sixties with no accusers to answer or social ambitions to protect move to reopen a forty-year-old scandal?

And why, I asked of the dirty street in general, did it take nine months to find the damn plane? I knew something of the state of New Jersey, having been born there, and I doubted that you could drop something as large as a plane there without killing one or two locals, never mind attracting their attention. Not even in 1941.

I decided to combine my lunch with a walk around Bryant Park. I stopped at a hotdog wagon near the northeast entrance. I was in line behind a thin office worker who cradled a large potted plant with one arm. She and the kid who ran the wagon were interacting socially.

"These things any good today?" she asked. "They fresh today?"

"Hey," the vendor said, "they're good every day. They're the same every day. They ever make you sick? They do, you come to me. I'll give you a seltzer. On the house. Hey, this guy with the long face wants to order. He looks hungry." I had been, anyway.

The park was an isolated bit of early fall. I walked its shaded stone paths, studying the shedding sycamores and the people beneath them. All but one of the broad flat benches were occupied by different generations of worn old men. The odd bench held Marilyn, or rather, she held the bench. The remains of her lunch guarded her left flank and a small pile of books secured the right. She was reading a newspaper pressed flat on her knees.

Her hair shone in the patch of sunlight she was using for her reading. For the first time, its random barrettes and conflicting bangs made sense to me, like an abstract viewed from the right distance. I didn't often see Marilyn under a noonday sun. Her post was in the dusty, artificial light of the New York Public Library, where she worked as a research assistant. Marilyn was my contact in the library, and her talent for research had made up for my lack of training on more than one occasion.

She was also my friend. Whether we were really more than friends or at least on our way to becoming more was an issue I had often considered but not yet resolved. Certainly we were sometime lovers, but in those days it was possible to obtain that status on very short acquaintance. That had been the case for us. Marilyn had initiated our relationship after we had known each other professionally for only a few weeks, and she had kept our affair casual and physical and intermittent. I think she'd been made cautious at the first by some details I'd let slip of my earlier, checkered career. Things were improving between us by the time I first heard of William Carteret. I'd convinced us both by then that I really was a stable, uninspired plodder. Marilyn seemed to admire those qualities.

I admired any number of Marilyn's qualities. She was hardworking, intelligent, and funny. I found her sense of humor refreshing because it lacked the self-deprecating edge of my own. Marilyn was unselfconscious to an extreme degree, which made her a straightforward person and an uncomplicated lover. The absence of self-doubt also gave her a quality in common with Harry, the certain knowledge of what she was doing and where she was going. It was a trait that never failed to surprise and impress me. Even her shortcomings were interesting novelties to me. She disliked doubt in others. She rejected all romance, and she was almost intolerant of impracticality and complication. Once I would have been willing to argue with her simple world view, but now I was dazed enough by my past failures to accept it and even to be comforted by it.

I stopped short of Marilyn's bench for a longer look. I'd come too close now for the thick auburn hair. Despite the flattering sunlight, it looked again its incongruous self, a mismatch of medium and message. Beneath it, Marilyn's face was a simpler study. I'd already decided that the heavy, shining eyebrows and the broad cheekbones indicated strength. I'd also noted that her thin, pale lips saved that strength from being misjudged, giving the whole collection an ascetic edge. I'd been careful, however, to keep this last observation to myself.

I stood there long enough admiring the view to break into her reading.

"Hello, Keane," she said. I was pleased to see that she smiled.

"Hello," I said. "What are you reading about?"

"The Jets. I needed a break from Hegel."

"I understand."

"Are you still in the Rockies?"

"No. I've been replaced. I wasn't sifting fast enough."

"That's too bad."

"You look like you've gotten some sun," I said, in an attempt to change the subject. I was on my lunch hour after all.

"I went beach walking," Marilyn said.

"Jersey?"

"Long Island. What's your new project?"

"Long Island, and New Jersey, too, in a way."

"Doesn't sound exciting." She folded her paper carefully and placed it under her pile of books.

"If I wanted excitement, I'd move to California."

"To be a detective?" she asked, teasing me.

"To roller-skate," I said.

She laughed at that mental image. "What do you want?" she asked.

"To bring order to disorder."

She expressed her opinion of that sort of remark with a grimace. "I meant from the library, Keane."

"I'm just going to read some old newspapers. This is a social conversation. I may need your help tomorrow, though."

"I'll look forward to seeing you," she said, rather too formally.

"Thank you," I replied.

"The fat end of your tie should be longer than the skinny end."

"Thank you very much."

As I continued my walk through the park, I considered my friendship with Marilyn, wondering again if we might have a future together. As usual, I came down solidly on both sides of the question. Opposites attract, I told myself. Yes, but did Marilyn know just how opposite we really are? Or were we? I'd changed my spots, hadn't I? Or was I just fooling someone, and, if so, whom? The answer to the last question should have come to me readily from long experience. I had never succeeded in fooling anyone but Mr. Owen Keane.

THREE

THE FRONT STEPS of my library were crowded with lunchers, a few of whom were watching a sidewalk juggler. He wore whiteface and a top hat and his location was better than his act. I climbed the worn center stairs, sidestepping aggressive pigeons. In the cool white marble foyer that was my favorite part of the building, I paused for a moment to talk with a guard. The Yankees were on their way to a new dynasty, the guard told me. The Tigers were washed up. I'd once made the mistake of telling him I followed Detroit.

The stairs that led me to the third floor were also formal white stone, but each step was disfigured by a yellow safety stripe painted on its edge. The misdeeds of recent generations confronted me again on the third floor. Elaborate stone stanchions ended in clusters of naked light bulbs. The ornate wood- and stonework of the walls and curved ceiling was disfigured by bright billboard murals that looked like the products of a depression-era work project.

I stopped at Fort Apache, Marilyn's name for the square grouping of counters in the catalog room that was home base for research assistants. I knew one or two of her coworkers well enough for a brief hello. Another guard waved me into the North Hall through a doorway adorned with a fatuous quote from Milton. Among its other functions, the North Hall was the main reading room. I passed rows of long reading tables lit by pale green living room lamps and occupied by other searchers. Ten-foot bookcases lined the walls beneath the open windows. Smaller cases and odd bits of furniture formed cul-de-sacs to my right. There was still no urgency in my progress, and I stopped once or twice during my walk through the hall to examine odd titles that caught my eye.

I'd decided to start with the newspaper accounts. The *New York Times Index* was kept near an exit at the far end of the room. The fat brown volume for 1941 was subtitled, "Master-Key to the News." And skeleton key to the Carterets, I hoped.

The bank was the first Carteret listed. It was hard to tell that 1941 had been anything but a good year for Carteret Federal. The only trace of its lost president was the story of his "election," noted between an estate lawsuit and the purchase of a new building. The presidential piece was repeated under William's own listing, along with his engagement announcement and the first mention of my assignment: "Carteret, W., and companion missing on NY-Albany flight, Oct 12, 19:7." It seemed to me that column seven of page nineteen was pretty casual coverage.

The follow-up stories came at four days and a week: "air search fruitless, Oct 14, 11:2; elopement possibility, Oct 17, 9:6." The final item for the year was run a full month after the disappearance: "no word from Carteret and companion, Nov 11, 32:4."

I noted the stories and traded the shelf for the 1942 edition. The bank had appointed Carl Vernia as acting president in January. The first item under its former president's listing sounded like a Sunday feature: "where is William Carteret? Apr 4, 49:2." The second and third supplied the answer: "Carteret plane, two bodies found, Jul 3, 9:1; missing fliers identified, Jul 5, 12:6.'' The *Times* ran Carteret's obituary on the same day his body was identified. Well, he had given them plenty of warning.

The *Times* microfilm was kept in brown cabinets protected by another counter and guarded by two more hourly workers. The younger of the two was named Phil. I knew him because he stood out. In a world of short sleeves, Phil wore a blue woolen blazer, day in and day out, a uniform for a branch of service I didn't recognize. I don't know why I stood out for him, but he greeted me by nodding his head and pushing his heavy horn-rims back up the slope of his nose. As always, he gave me the impression that I was holding him up.

"Don't worry about a slip," he said. "Just tell me what you need."

I gave Phil my shopping list. He hurried off and returned quickly with an armful of small cardboard boxes.

"Easy to find those 1941 reels," he said. "December of '41 stands out like a sore thumb."

"It does?" I prompted politely.

"Popular item. Pearl Harbor stuff. People have worn the damn box out. These boxes are all brown, see? They're originals. The Pearl Harbor box is a replacement. It's white."

"Huh." Phil's shoptalk reminded me of an earlier remark, Harry's suggestion that the war had stolen the spotlight from a flying playboy's disappearance. It was the most obvious explanation of the restrained coverage. For that reason alone, I didn't fully believe it.

I settled in for the afternoon at a photocopying microfilm viewer with my stack of brown boxes and a pocketful of dimes. There was an older man with a bristled chin at the station next to me. A short man peered over his shoulder as he squeaked through a film that, I gathered, contained the daily from the day the old man had been born. The notation of his birth, which he eventually found and proudly read aloud, couldn't have told him as much as his driver's license. Its attraction must have been that his name had been recorded in a daily newspaper. At the moment, that medium spoke more to me of mortality than of immortality.

Thinned of redundant details, the newspaper articles I'd listed told me the following story.

October 12, 1941

William Carteret and a companion have been reported missing on a Long Island to Albany flight, according to a spokesman for Carteret Federal Bank. The Carteret plane, a blue-and-white Monocoupe cabin monoplane, was last seen over Great Bay on October 10. No sighting or report has been received since.

Mr. Carteret, a noted amateur aviator, assumed the presidency of the bank in February. Tentative plans call for a vigorous air search of the Hudson River valley.

October 14, 1941

...Mr. Carteret's companion has been identified as his fiancée, Miss Lynn Baxter, of Westpark, Albany....the activities of nine searching planes have produced no results.... Mr. Francis Baxter reported the plane overdue on Saturday night...airfields within the calculated range of the plane have been contacted.

October 17, 1941

...the possibility of an elopement has not been ruled out, according to Carteret Federal spokesman Mr. Carl Vernia.

November 11, 1941

...still missing one month to the day their small plane left Great Bay on a flight to Albany. Civil Aeronautics authorities reported no results from an extensive air search...last seen on October 10, at approximately 11:15 A.M. by members of the Carteret household staff...numerous false reports have been received, one of which placed the plane as far west as Chicago...Carteret completed several cross-country endurance flights in 1938...in the company of Mr. Harry Greb he won the Millar Cup Miami to Bahamas Air Race.

July 3, 1942

The Monocoupe cabin plane belonging to missing banker William Carteret was found yesterday by two soldiers from Fort Dix. The wreckage, located nine miles east of Bargersville, New Jersey, contained two bodies, believed to be those of Mr. Carteret and his fiancée, Miss Lynn Baxter.

Privates Paul Demerast and Thomas Wozniak

reported stumbling upon the wreckage in the dense undergrowth of the pine forest.

July 5, 1942

...positively identified...death, in the opinion of the coroner, was instantaneous.

So much for the story the *Times* had told the world. It gave me a few new details: the approximate time of the last sighting, the type of plane, the approximate crash site, the names of the men who found it, and Carl Vernia's contemporary involvement. Not very much. No mention of sabotage and no explanation for the change in flight plan. If Robert was the Howard Hughes of Long Island, William had been the Amelia Earhart.

The only really important thing I'd found was the name of the other victim. Lynn Baxter. Suddenly she was a person, not just some appendage of Carteret's. I found myself wondering what she had been like. She had had a father who had worried about her when the plane had failed to appear. That was all I knew. I added her name to my short list of research subjects.

I pushed back my chair and stretched my eyes. The wall above the bookcases to my left was the only restful view in the North Hall. It was plain stone block and water stained and too uncomplicated for my present state of mind. I leaned back and studied the ceiling, instead. I followed its intricate red-and-gold-and-green pattern, without finding a beginning or an end. It led me past the large painting in the center of the ceiling. Age and water spots had left it indecipherable. When my neck began to ache instead of my eyes, I went back to studying the viewer.

A picture of William accompanied each story, usually with an airplane for a backdrop. The picture next to his obituary was a formal, president-of-the-bank picture. His hair was extremely short and parted high, and his thin nose gave his narrow face a sharp, angular look. William's age had not been given in any of the stories, and his photographs had led me to estimate it at about thirty. His obituary told me he'd been only twenty-six at the time of his death. The difference wasn't great, but it suggested the possibility of a closer relationship between the two Carteret brothers.

In addition to his age, his obituary told me that William had been "prepared" at Fenbroke Military Academy in upstate New York and had graduated from Cornell in 1936. There was also a list of his activities as an aviator, the number of which suggested that he'd taken his undergraduate degree in barnstorming. Finally, I learned that his mother, about whom I'd been told nothing, had passed away in 1927.

Lynn Baxter's obituary appeared next to Carteret's. It seemed sadder than his because it was so brief. They were all still characters in a story to me, but Lynn Baxter, my newest name, seemed especially shadowy and ill defined. She'd been only twenty-two at the time of the crash. The daughter of Mr. and Mrs. Francis Baxter had attended the Marie Walker School of Elmsbury, New York, graduated from Smith, and become engaged to William Carteret. There was nothing else, not even a photograph.

I remembered then that I had found a mention of Carteret's engagement announcement in the *Times*

Index. I switched microfilm reels and cranked my way to the story. There I found what I was hoping for, a picture of Lynn Baxter, under the quaint heading "Becomes Affianced." Hers was a pensive engagement picture. Her hair was blond and shoulder length, parted simply on one side. Her face was attractive, but without an expressive mouth for support, it seemed to fall away from her broad forehead and large eyes. Her dark eyes saved her for me, kept her from being a minor character. Their glance passed over my shoulder, looking toward a new marriage and an uncertain future with an expression that made the whole business real to me. She seemed anxious.

My newspaper reading took me hours longer than I'd expected. I found I couldn't page through the microfilms without stopping to read about the war. The Germans had been closing on Moscow when my subjects were first reported missing. The *Times* ran a small map each day showing the progress of the advance. Its broken lines and arrows reduced the war to the level of a television weather map. The sinking of the *Ruben James* had captured the headlines at about the time Carteret's plane had been missing for a month. The same page that told of the discovery of the wreck also carried a story of General Eisenhower inspecting U.S. troops in Scotland. I wondered if Private Robert Carteret had been among them.

My eyes were sore. The microfilm viewer, which couldn't hold the full breadth of a blown-up page and required constant lateral shifts, had given me a headache. I also had the feeling that I was wasting my time. Innocent or guilty, Robert Carteret already knew more about the crash than squeaking microfilms could ever tell me. I decided to call it a day.

I thought I would dream of the Carterets that night. I lucked out and dreamed of Marilyn instead.

FOUR

I WENT DIRECTLY from my apartment to the library the next morning, which allowed me to sleep in. My biographical research hadn't touched Charles Carteret or his surviving son, so I knew my morning's work would be less than exciting. I promised myself as I rode the subway that this would be my last visit to the microfilm. As old as William Carteret's story was, I still hoped there was something to be learned outside of the New York Public Library.

First, though, I stopped in the catalog room, with only the vaguest sense of business. Marilyn stood behind the high counter that protected the research assistants, sorting slips of yellow paper and white paper. Her smile, when she looked up, was all business as mechanical as her sorting.

"Good morning," she said, "what have you brought me?"

Marilyn's ability to assume a professional posture that overrode our personal relationship always gave her a subtle moral advantage over me. It also irritated me, reminding me, unhappily, of Harry's Mrs. Kiefner. I mentally shifted gears during my last two steps to the counter and affected a professional air myself.

"I need some direction, Ms. Tucci," I said. "I need to find the record of an inquiry into a plane crash that occurred in 1941. The plane crashed in Jersey, but the flight originated on Long Island. I don't know if I want the FAA or some local agency or where in our wonderful city I would go to find out.''

''You certainly cover a range,'' she said.

''I have to visit the *Times* microfilm. I shouldn't be more than half an hour.''

''I'll see what I can come up with.''

''Fine.''

''Is something wrong, Keane?'' she asked.

''No,'' I said. In fact, I was put out by our impersonal exchange and my inability to operate above it. ''Why do you ask?''

''You called me Ms. Tucci. You haven't called me that in a long time.''

''I don't think you've ever called me Owen.''

''Does anybody?''

''I'll be back in thirty minutes.''

The *Times Obituary Index* was in use, so I pulled the general index for 1940 and looked under ''Deaths.'' Charles, father of William and Robert, had passed away on or about September 21. As I wrote that reference down in my notebook a page of the index slipped from under my thumb. When I looked back, I saw the subject heading ''Debutantes,'' and below it an item ''Baxter, Lynn, Jan 15, 29:1.'' Eureka, indeed. I'd learned enough about serious research to capitalize on luck. I noted the reference, hoping I'd find another photograph, and went to see Phil, guardian of the microfilm.

Charles Carteret's obituary repeated the vague picture of him that Harry had sketched without really filling it in. Carteret had been in and out of minor public offices since the turn of the century. Although he was only a small bank financier, he seemed to be well connected. His family had settled on the right part of the Hudson, too. I decided that I could assume considerable influence surrounding the family and the bank, even after Charles's death. Enough influence to have exempted one son from military service or to have downplayed the disappearance of the other.

My hunch on the debutante story paid off. It was accompanied by a gallery of portraits, including one of Lynn Baxter. She appeared in a full-length photograph intended to display her heavy-looking, angular gown. She was smiling in this picture and looked almost beautiful. In a way, that disappointed me, made me less sure that this woman, dead forty years, somehow needed my help. I scanned the article describing the women who had come of age at the Waldorf that night. Lynn's brief mention could have been the first draft of her obituary, except for the last four words: "escorted by Robert Carteret."

At that moment I felt like a detective in some book of my youth, stumbling upon a half-burnt note in a garden. Had I been reading the Carteret story in a paperback, the presence of two brothers and a girl would immediately have suggested a triangle. As it was, I'd thought Lynn Baxter at most a bystander to the brothers' rivalry. Now it seemed she might have been both cause and victim.

I spent a dime for a record of my discovery and turned the films over to the file clerk. My next stop was current biography. In *Who's Who in American Banking,* Carlyle and Smith, 1980, I found the following brief entry.

CARTERET, ROBERT CHARLES; (b) NYC, Apr 11, 1917; (s) Charles & Mary (Farrell); (e) Fenbroke M.A. 1934, Cornell U. 1938; Chief

Executive Officer Carteret Federal Bank, 1945;
U.S. Army Infantry 1941-44; NY Athletic Club,
Great Bay Country Club, Delta Kappa Epsilon.

Carteret's retiring nature prompted me to read a great
deal into the slight traces I found. But for the name
and the dates the sketch could have been written for
William Carteret.

The *Obituary Index* was free. I looked up Carl Vernia and bothered Phil for the last time. Vernia's obituary told me that he'd died of a heart attack in his
home on Long Island. He and the century had been
the same age: forty-one when he'd assumed the presidency and sixty-eight when he'd died. The writer described Vernia as the "architect of the Carteret
Corporation, its president and chairman of the
board." Robert Carteret may be lazy, I thought, but
he knows how to delegate. Vernia was survived by "his
daughter, Carolyn Vernia, commercial loan officer
with the bank." Harry had been right, I decided. Loan
officer to president in five years suggested a formida-
ble personality. There was still the possibility of inter-
vention by Carteret, who might have owed the Vernia
family a debt, but I was more inclined to give Carolyn the benefit of the doubt. The photograph of her
father that had run with his obituary looked like it had
been cropped from a larger grouping. His face was
masked by heavy glasses and a blank expression. It
was an unsatisfying illustration for a character I'd already cast as a major player.

Carl Vernia was so unsatisfying, in fact, that I
turned off the viewer and thought instead of the relationship between Robert Carteret and Lynn Baxter. I

must have been looking proud of myself. Marilyn read my expression as she came down the aisle.

"You've found something," she said.

"I'm making progress. How did you do with the FAA?"

"The CAB, you mean, Civil Aeronautics Board. The FAA didn't come along until 1967. In 1941 the Board was part of the Department of Commerce. You want the records of the Safety Bureau, Accident Investigation Division, New York Office. The old CAB records are kept at the Federal Records Building on East Thirty-fourth Street."

"Did you write any of that down?"

"I even used block letters."

"Thank you," I said.

"Are you going to tell me what this is all about?" Marilyn asked.

"I can't now. I've got to stay on the trail while it's still warm."

"This trail has been cold for forty years, Keane."

"Owen," I said.

"Would you like to come over for dinner tonight?"

"Owen?"

"Owen."

"Yes. I'll come."

"Seven o'clock. Bring white wine with a cork. And here, I copied this."

"This" was an article entitled "Safety Sleuths" from the March 1943 edition of *Flying*.

"You cover a lot of ground yourself," I said. "Thanks."

I found the day outside overcast and a little cool, but I felt strangely elated. I've always felt that a low gray sky does something positive for New York City, making its own cold grayness seem less unnatural. Of course, my mood now was due to more than the sky. I was out of the library for the moment, and I'd been asked to dinner. I'd been invited to dinner at Marilyn's often enough to know that eating would be low on the agenda, so I treated myself to a large roast beef sandwich.

Over lunch I read the article Marilyn had given me. An excerpt from the second paragraph will convey the tone: "These junk-pile Sherlocks have been trained to get the answers to the numerous questions that inevitably arise when planes succumb to the uninvited wooing of gravity." Besides suggesting a wartime shortage of writers, the story described the government's early attempts to scientifically explain a plane crash from whatever physical evidence remained. It also confirmed that the investigators for a New Jersey crash would have come from New York City. If specialists in a particular aircraft component or type of plane were needed, they would have tapped the Washington headquarters.

The Federal Records Building was a large pseudo-Roman structure of dirty limestone. A Latin inscription over the main entrance challenged my rising mood: *Nil homini certum est.* Nothing is sure to man. Inside, the main corridor was high and drafty. Its vaulted ceiling was decorated in mosaics made of thousands of tiny tiles. Their intricacy made me think of an age of careful craftsmanship and a painfully low hourly wage. A pensioner dressed as a guard directed me down a worn stone stairway. Everything about the place suggested living history, which heartened me. I'd begun to despair of any record's surviving forty years of bureaucratic reshuffling.

Ovid's warning came back to me when I opened the pebbled glass door marked "Department of Transportation, Division of Records." The office contradicted the rest of the building, with earthtone carpeting and an acoustical ceiling. To my left a young woman was typing quietly at a keyboard connected to a CRT. An older woman faced me across a Formica counter. Her iron gray hair was shorter than mine and her glasses hung on a gold chain around her neck. The heavy rings on her fingers suggested cocktails. A nameplate on the counter read "Mrs. Peiffer." I approached the counter wearing my brightest researcher smile.

"Hello," I said, "I wonder if I might see a Civil Aeronautics Board report on a plane crash that occurred in 1941?"

"What month?" Mrs. Peiffer asked.

"October. The wreck was found in July 1942."

"Where?"

"New Jersey."

"A plane crashed in 1941, in New Jersey, and nobody found it for a year?"

"Nine months," I said.

"Huh. Write down your name and address. You have a pen?"

"Do you need the nearest town or the pilot's name?" I asked.

"No, thank you."

She left me marveling at filing in the computer age. I turned to examine a yellowed engraving that seemed to be trying to link the office with its building, but I was interrupted by a discreet cough. Mrs. Peiffer's ringed fingers clanked on a small tin box of the type used for filing index cards.

"Here you go," she said.

"Microfilm?" I asked, my heart sinking.

"Fiche," Mrs. Peiffer replied. "Microfiche. The last six months of 1942. The index for each sheet is in the upper-left-hand corner. The viewer is through that door."

The records had indeed survived their agency, but in a fossilized form. Each of the negativelike sheets held several hundred pages. I found the Carteret report on the third sheet and settled in for an afternoon of eyestrain. It had been issued on August 8, 1942. One month, give or take a long weekend, after the wreck had been found. I noted the investigators' names, wondering as I did so how long they'd been dead. All I have left of their brief effort are my elliptical notes.

...plane NC-4214, Monocoupe 372151-1938...registered to William Hobart Carteret, license no. 5641...nine miles east of Bargersville, New Jersey, twelve miles south of Smithtown, New Jersey...last seen over Great Bay, Long Island, October 10, 1941, 11:15 A.M. by P. T. Gregson, Carteret estate...wreckage contained two bodies identified as W. H. Carteret...Lynn Baxter, Albany...identification made by Ocean County Sheriff's Office...due to condition of bodies...exposure...massive head injuries...animals...identification made by clothing, jewelry...head injuries judged to be cause of death...death believed to be instantaneous...fuselage resting on left side...dense pine forest...left wing under the fuselage...right wing ten yards behind fuselage, along line of descent...tail assembly largely intact...no propeller strikes on trees or ground...magneto switches in off position...no evidence of fire...evidence of massive oil loss along right side of fuselage...oil filler cap not found at crash site...position of fuselage and damage to trees indicates a shallow path of descent...possibility of attempted "deadstick" landing...last regular maintenance performed on October 8, 1941...evidence of Gustave Warden, mechanic, Coram Airfield, Coram, Long Island...oil changed at that time...W. H. Carteret occasionally performed his own maintenance... Probable Cause: Engine failure due to massive oil loss, possibly caused by defective oil filler cap, resulted in uncontrolled descent over thickly wooded terrain... Aircraft Recommendations: None... Maintenance Recommendations: None... Recommendations for Additional Investigations: None.

Not a very inspired effort. Why, I wondered. I read the report several times, looking for the answer. I compared it to other reports on the same sheet. I read about a fiery crash of an airliner near Hartford that was blamed on a broken piece of tubing and a military plane downed on Long Island by birds. Those reports were more detailed than the Carteret investigation, but even they seemed like elaborate guesswork.

Eventually, Mrs. Peiffer appeared in the doorway and pointed to her watch. A half hour later she came in again and looked over my shoulder. "Did it take you nine months to find the report?" she asked.

"Sorry. I get carried away."

"I know what you mean," she said. "Sometimes I look at these old reports and wonder about the people who wrote them. I wonder what they would think if they could see them now." She reached around me and pulled the fiche out of the viewer. "These things don't wear out," she said. "That's what they tell me anyway. It's something to think about, your paperwork lasting forever." She switched off the viewer and shut the tin box with a final peal from her rings. "I wonder what they would have done if they'd known that?"

"Punched the clock and gone home," I said.

FIVE

MARILYN AND I SHARED Brooklyn. The borough had been the subject of our first talk. We were both foreigners in that exotic land, but we had reacted to the situation differently. Marilyn enjoyed exploring Brooklyn, learning to negotiate both its streets and its several ethnic personalities. I went there to sleep.

Marilyn's apartment building had been a middle-class bedroom a generation earlier, one of hundreds of a half dozen floors or so that still took in New York's workers at night. The best of that business had passed to the neighboring states, however, and the bedrooms of Brooklyn were sliding as a result. There was still some interesting architecture, the occasional cherub and balustrade and some names that hung on because they were fashioned in the stone: Ascot, Strand, Marlborough. Most of the buildings had fallen victim to their tenants and the times, but Marilyn's building, the Alhambra, was also the victim of its owners. The security door that opened to Marilyn's ring was plastic where it should have been glass. The lobby carpet was a garish green print and the cage elevator shaft had been encased in cheap paneling. I avoided the last offense by taking the narrow imitation marble stairs. The green carpet greeted me again on the third floor. It hid the gentle list of the hallway and gave the ancient woodwork a seasick glow.

Marilyn opened the door as I knocked. "Hello, Keane," she said. "You look beat."

"Thanks," I said. "It's this damn carpet. Let me in and I'll look much better. What happened to Owen, anyway?"

"I don't want you to get spoiled."

She backed up far enough for me to enter and close the door. I offered her the wine.

"Thank you," she said.

She was barefoot and perfumed and her ascetic lips were hidden under shining red. She was wearing a long wraparound skirt, which became her, lending her a grace that her usual businesslike movements lacked. Above the skirt she wore a leotard that became her almost literally.

She noted my inspection. "You like it?" she asked.

"It?"

"My outfit."

"Yes," I said, "I do."

She backed me a step toward the door.

"Marilyn," I said.

"Keane. Do you want to get crazy now or after we eat?"

"What are we having?"

"I think I have a can of tuna fish."

"I wouldn't count on after," I said.

"I don't count on anything." She grabbed my belt and pulled me toward her. "What's the matter? Would you like some wine first?"

"No," I said, "just hit me over the head with the bottle and drag me into the bedroom."

"You're usually not sarcastic till afterward. You're not having problems, are you?"

"Not yet. I haven't seen you to talk with in a month. I thought we could visit for a while."

"Dinner and talk." She shook her head. "Next time, you'll want a corsage. I'll open the wine. Sit down and tell me about your day."

I sat on an old sofa that shared the living room with a collection of plants and a stereo. "Not much to tell," I said, addressing a philodendron. "I spent most of the day sitting at a viewer."

Marilyn's reply echoed from the kitchen's depths. "The only time I saw you, you were staring up at the ceiling."

"Resting my eyes."

"Daydreaming. Tell me more about your assignment."

"I really can't discuss it. Tell me about this album," I said, picking one at random from the rack. "I don't recognize the group."

"I'm asking you out of politeness, Keane. You're not going to heighten my interest by playing coy." She came out of the kitchen carrying a tray. In addition to the bottle of wine and two glasses, the tray held a small plate.

"What's that?" I asked.

"Hors d'oeuvres," Marilyn said. An elaborate name for what appeared to be peanut butter on saltine crackers. "Sit down here on the rug. It'll be sort of a picnic."

"Sort of."

"Why don't you want to tell me about your job?"

That was a good question. I paused to consider it. I knew the Carteret business was already more to me than just another assignment. I decided that I wasn't being coy so much as protective. I didn't want Marilyn to casually dismiss my case as just another research project. So I stalled. "Why are you so interested?"

"It's research. I'm a research assistant. You come up with some things that are challenging. Go ahead and eat it," she said as I poked at one of her canapés. "Don't be such a damn cat."

"I think most of the things I get into are pretty dry," I said, between unsuccessful attempts to swallow peanut butter.

"There's no such thing as dry research, Keane," she said. "The subject doesn't matter. The job is digging out facts and figures, names and dates. Not being sloppy. Getting it right, and getting on to the next project."

That last tenet of the researcher's code seemed to remind her of something. "Finished your wine?" she asked, pulling me toward her with my tie.

"Marilyn."

"Take a long drink. You're about to be carried off kicking and screaming."

"Just yesterday I was admiring the spiritual cast of your face."

"So you're a lousy judge of character. That can't surprise you too much. Look, if it will make you happier, I won't enjoy it."

"That will certainly make me happier," I said.

We made love then, eventually working our way into the bedroom, the threat of canned tuna fish and the problem of the Carterets forgotten. Afterward, I played with her silly hair while she lay with closed eyes. Somewhere nearby a stereo was being played for the benefit of the entire block. Aretha Franklin was singing a sad song about lonely people and the hopeless dreams only they understand. Her music was out of step with my current mood, which was unusually happy and hopeful, a result of both Marilyn's attentions and my new assignment. It was a nice mood while it lasted.

"You seem fascinated by my hair," Marilyn said after a time.

"I am. It's fascinating hair."

"Just don't tell me it's beautiful."

"I won't. I've been well trained."

I was half asleep when Marilyn stirred herself. She rested her head on my chest and waited. I waited, too. A moment later she prodded me in the ribs. "Come on, Keane," she said. "Tell me about your project."

"I'm a confidential agent."

"Omit details."

"A hopeless strategy, as you are the superior researcher. You could probably reconstruct my two days' work by checking the lint in my pants cuffs."

"If you had cuffs on your pants I wouldn't be sleeping with you."

"The problem is," I said, "you're not sleeping."

"I need you to tell me a story. Unsatisfied women have a lot of nervous energy." She demonstrated that law of nature by poking at my ribs again.

"Let's talk about our relationship," I said.

"That word has too many syllables to describe us. Let's tell me about your project."

I was still jealous of my secret, but I was too tired to make a sound decision. "It seems there were two brothers," I began. "Bob and Bill. They were only a couple years apart. I like to think they grew up pals, befriended each other in the isolation of their family's money."

"But you don't know."

"I thought you wanted a story."

"But not a fairy tale."

I ignored that pointed warning. "Bob, who was younger, did everything Bill did, went to the same schools, belonged to the same clubs. They were two close brothers."

"T-o-o close?"

"That also. Then Bill turned the tables and imitated Bob. He became engaged to Bob's girl. And he inherited the family fortune."

"At the same time?"

"Maybe he inherited first."

"She doesn't sound very nice."

"I think of her as a nice person in a tough spot."

"Based on what information? How much of this are you making up?"

"I'm a reaearcher," I started to say, but Marilyn cut me off.

"This doesn't sound like any research project I ever heard of." She sat up. When I reached out to her, she intercepted my hand and held it away from her. "What was the girl's name?" she asked.

"Lynn. She and Bill took off in an airplane..."

"It crashed in New Jersey. I know this part. Bob sawed the wing off, right?"

Marilyn was suddenly angry, which took me by surprise. I had been worried that she would dismiss my story or belittle it. Somehow, it had offended her.

"So who are you working for?" she demanded. "Bob?"

"I'm sleepy," I said.

"What does he want, a scrapbook?"

"You sleepy yet?"

"I'm disappointed."

"It's only a story," I said, betraying my own hopes.

"I'm disappointed in you. If you're going to live in a fantasy world, why don't you make it a nicer one?"

"What do you mean by that?"

She released my hand. "I think you should give this assignment to someone else. I don't think it's good for you."

That statement reduced me to a stunned silence. Every detective is sooner or later warned off a case, but the threat is usually delivered by a thug or a crooked cop, not by a friend.

Marilyn lay down with her back to me. Outside, Aretha had changed songs, and she and I were now in sync. She was asking where her lover had gone.

"Marilyn," I said.

I saw her back stiffen. I thought for a moment that she would ask me to leave. Instead she said: "I'm sleepy now, Keane."

"Owen," I said.

SIX

BREAKFAST WAS BETTER than dinner. I ate scrambled eggs mixed with crumbled matzo and a bagel still warm from the oven while sitting alone at a tiny table in a crowded delicatessen.

Marilyn never felt like eating in the morning. On that particular morning she hadn't even felt like speaking. She'd looked at me as though I were an overdue book she'd found under the covers. I'd told myself the wine had given her a hangover. In any case, I'd left her apartment without challenge or comment.

I went to the office to report, but Harry had gone to Boston. Ms. Kiefner was too busy running the staff around to notice my presence, so I sat down to organize my notes.

I decided that I'd accomplished little more than corroborating Mr. Ohlman's recollections. My only genuine discovery, Robert Carteret's relationship with Lynn Baxter, was an additional strike against my "client." It also made Lynn look less than innocent, as Marilyn had noted, and that bothered me. For the moment I decided not to let that piece of the puzzle fall into its obvious place.

I'd done little to make real people of my names from the past, beyond romanticizing them. I had discovered surprising similarities in the backgrounds of the two sons. I wondered if Charles Carteret had purposely raised an heir and a replacement. I wrote "spare heir" on the margin of my notebook. The ambitious father may have overlooked the possibility of an equally ambitious second son.

It occurred to me that I might be making too much of their upbringing, depending too much on my own experiences and feelings as a second son. In my case there had been no grooming for wealth or anything else. My natural inclination had been to do everything differently than my older brother had, to be everything that he was not. What form would that natural rivalry have taken for brothers who were so close—"t-o-o" close—and who were allowed so little freedom? How would that same force push them apart after the death of their father?

I sat, during my speculation, with my eyes closed and my feet on my small metal desk. My scant notes spread before me had been left far behind. Having failed to flesh out my principals through research, I had begun the process in my mind, without benefit of substantiation.

Charles Carteret: Old for the task of raising his sons. Too old or too sentimental to have remarried. Without sympathy for his sons as individuals. Driven to perpetuating a family name at the expense of that family.

William Carteret; Heir apparent. Raised to a conventional mark but expressing unconventionality in the appropriate medium of his day, flying. Bank president for less than a year. Had he been flying toward something or away?

Robert Carteret: Longer lived than his brother but less well defined. Without William to break ground for him, Robert's development seemed to have stopped, as though he depended for his definition on his brother, as I depended on Harry. Thesis and antithesis.

Marilyn was right, my job did involve fantasy. Her mistake was deciding that meant an unreal world. No researcher would deal with a world, however fantastic, that was unreal. No detective would. That would be a pointless investigation, what my friend Raymond Chandler called "spillikens in the parlor." I knew I had no great talent for research, aside from a normal amount of luck. But I did have a capacity for fantasy, an ability to see beyond the actual to the possible. That, I decided, more than anything else, suited me for my work.

I realized as I returned to my notebook that what I needed was a living witness. I wanted some bridge between this case and the 1981 in which I had to live. The most obvious candidate was Robert Carteret. Harry hadn't specifically told me not to contact him. I knew, of course, that it had simply never occurred to him. I also had the names of the CAB investigators and those of the two soldiers who had found the wreck. Finding that group would require the FBI. That left whatever Baxters still lived in Albany and Gustave Warden, the plane's mechanic.

I dialed information and asked for the number of the Coram Airfield. The operator's reply caught me without a pencil ready. I was actually nervous as I punched the number, as though I were calling Marilyn for a return bout.

A girl with a pleasant voice answered with the name "Coram."

I asked for Gustave Warden.

"Senior or Junior?"

"Senior."

She was gone for an unexplained moment or two.

"He's in the middle of a job," she finally said. "Can he call you back?"

I told her I'd call again in an hour and rang off. Almost immediately, I had a better idea. In fifteen minutes, when Ms. Kiefner departed for coffee, I presented myself at the desk of her assistant, Mr. Pulsifer's nominal secretary, and requested a car. As I'd cleverly anticipated, she handed me a voucher without any expression of interest.

The attendant in the garage across the street was a stocky Italian named Tommy who had a passion for Sherlock Holmes that I'd come to regret. He laid his *Daily News* aside when I stepped up to his booth.

"Here's one for you," he said in greeting. "How high was the elm Holmes found at Hurlstone Estates?"

"He only found the stump. The tree had been struck by lightning."

"God damn it. I suppose you read it last night."

"How about a car? It doesn't have to be the third in line."

"Very funny. How high had the tree been? Answer that."

"Sixty-four feet," I said.

"God damn it," Tommy replied.

The midmorning traffic was light. I reached Coram about the time of my promised second call. The town was small and defined by sparsely wooded hills. A gas station attendant directed me to the Coram Airfield.

A single paved runway divided a grassy field. The lone building was actually two hangars joined, old to new. The old section was a long series of cinder block stalls sharing a tin roof. Each stall contained a small plane, two or three of which were surrounded by tall weeds. The newer section was an aluminum prefab. The glass door I entered read "Coram Aviation."

A teenage brunette behind a low counter said her "May I help you?" exactly as she had over the phone.

"My name is Owen Keane. I'd like to speak with Gustave Warden, please. I called about an hour ago."

"You'd better call him Mr. Warden or Gus," she said.

"What do you call him?" I asked.

"Grandad."

She pointed to a door behind her. In the cool open space beyond, there were several light planes. Gus Warden emerged from behind one as my steps sounded on the concrete. He was oddly like the mental image I'd been building of him: short and stocky with a weathered face and a thinning white crew cut. He wiped his hands on a piece of rag as I approached, although his khaki overalls testified to regular transgressions. He smiled and extended his hand, and I thought that his granddaughter had come by her openness honestly.

"Gus Warden," he said. "What can I do for you?"

I repeated my name and the three of my firm. "I'd like to ask you some questions," I said.

"You got a card?" Warden asked.

I dug in my wallet for a business card that didn't have a Library of Congress call number scrawled across it. Warden considered the card briefly before filing it away.

"What's this about?" He was less friendly now.

"William Carteret." For some reason I knew that brief reference would be enough.

"Huh," Warden said. "You mind walking a little? I've been working on an overhaul on that Yankee." He pointed to a squat plane in the corner. "I haven't straightened my legs since eight o'clock this morning."

We started across the grass toward a barbed wire fence that marked the edge of the field.

"How the hell did William Carteret surface again?" Warden asked.

"My firm has been asked to look into his death."

"Who asked, or can you say?"

"I'm really not supposed to."

"Fine. Hell, I haven't even thought of the guy in years. What do you want to hear?"

"How well did you know him?"

"Better than you might think, with him being filthy rich. I knew Harry Greb, a professional pilot Carteret would hire to hold his hand on long hauls. And of course I worked on the *Phaeton*."

"The *Phaeton*?"

"I haven't thought of that in years either. That was the name of Carteret's plane. They all had nicknames back then. It was a Monocoupe, a great little plane. They didn't build too many of them. Too rich for most people's blood, and too hard to fly. All engine, you know. I haven't seen one in donkey's years. Carteret took good care of his, wasn't afraid to get his hands dirty, but most of the engine work was beyond him. That Warner radial was a handful."

We walked in silence for a time while Warden thought back. He moved with a slow, rolling gait on his short stiff legs.

"Yeah, I knew Carteret," Warden finally said. "Not that I called him Billy or anything, but he'd talk my ear off during an overhaul."

"What did he talk about?"

"Flying. Cars. Women. He was sowing his wild oats in those days. Got them in just in time."

We paused to watch a small single-engine plane bounce past us on the runway.

"Student," Warden said. "My son's an instructor."

"You worked on the *Phaeton* two days before the accident?"

"You done your homework. Yeah. Routine inspection. Hundred hour, probably. There was nothing wrong with that engine."

"Do you remember much about the accident?"

"I remember being mad and a little scared. I'd never been involved in anything like that before. Those federals put the fear of God in me. But hell, they knew there was nothing wrong with that engine."

"Then what caused the crash?" I asked.

Warden stopped walking and looked me in the eye. "You know the last time I worked on the plane and you don't know what caused the crash? Am I supposed to believe that? You're not as smooth as the detectives on television."

"I'm not a detective," I said.

He turned to resume our walk. "It was no big secret. He lost all his goddamn oil. It must have looked like a gusher coming out of that cowling. The engine would have seized in no time flat, so Carteret shut it down. If he hadn't it might have thrown the prop, and then they could have just kissed it good-bye. As it was, Carteret had a chance to bring it down in one piece.

But that old Monocoupe didn't have much wing for its weight, meaning that as a glider it was pretty much a brick. Plus he must have had oil all over his windshield. One tough spot to be in. Harry Greb might have pulled it off. I don't know.

"Like I said, it was no big secret why the plane went down. The problem was explaining how the oil got out in the first place. The Feds couldn't tie it to a busted line or gasket."

We'd reached the fence. Warden looked across the neighboring field to the bare white skeleton of a new house. "Two days after it's done they'll be complaining about the traffic in the pattern," he said.

"The CAB report mentioned that the oil filler cap was missing," I said.

Warden chuckled. "You remember that part, huh? Well, that cap being gone isn't the answer. It's the mystery." He pointed to the runway where the little trainer was making another shaky pass. "That student out there barely knows which side of an airplane is up, but he knows enough to check his oil during preflight. Hell, it's the only thing some of them do check. And after they check it, they snug that filler cap on so tight the next guy needs a pipe wrench to get it off."

"Carteret could still have forgotten," I said.

"I'll never believe it," Warden said, "and I'll tell you why. If he'd left that cap off during his preflight, he wouldn't have gotten into the air before he noticed his oil spewing out. And if he was blind and did take off, he wouldn't have gotten far. Hell, that airplane flew at least a hundred miles that day. No way that cap was missing when it took off."

We started back to the hangar. "How did the cap come off then?" I asked.

Warden started to shrug my question off. Then he smiled. "It's ancient history now, so I guess it couldn't hurt to speculate a little.

"I didn't have idea one at the time of the crash," Warden said. "Then the Japs bombed Pearl Harbor, and I landed in the air corps working on P-47s in England. I was listening to some hangar talk one night when I heard something that made me think of William Carteret. Some old hands were talking about the different ways you could sabotage an airplane. One of the guys mentioned pouring water in the oil."

Warden turned to face me. He was still smiling. I sensed that he was pleased to have an audience for his story after so many years. "It was supposed to work like this. You pour a cup or two of water into the engine oil. No problem. The engine runs fine. Nothing happens till it heats up real good. Then the water starts to turn to steam. You still can't tell that anything's wrong by looking at the engine gages. Oil pressure looks great and the temperature's normal. The steam builds up until something gives. If you have a weak line, it'll part. If the engine connections are solid, the filler cap will fire off like a rocket. Half of your oil is in your face before you know what hit you. Sound familiar?"

"Why didn't the federal investigators come up with that?" I asked.

"I can't help you there. For all I know, they did. I was yanked into the service pretty quick, like I said."

I judged that Warden's moment of nostalgia was passing, so I hurried my questioning. "Why did Carteret fly south?"

"That's the other big mystery, and nobody's going to give you the answer. Since I'm guessing today I'd say it was Carteret's last fling. He hadn't been a businessman very long at the time, but he had a life of it to look forward to. I think he just decided to take the weekend off."

"And elope?"

"Elope or screw the hell around. You'd be surprised how hot we got in the forties. Well, I've got to get back to work, if you've asked everything."

"I've one more question, if you don't mind. Could you tell me the best road to Great Bay?"

"Simple enough. You want to see if the Carteret place is still there?"

"It is. Robert Carteret still lives in it."

"Huh. I forgot about him."

"Did you know Robert?"

"I met him. He was a lot less flashy than his brother, quieter."

"He still is," I said.

"I wonder if he still has his license."

"Pilot's license?" I asked.

"Hell yes. That's how I met him. He used to fly the *Phaeton* over here sometimes, or pick it up."

"Did he pick it up that last time?"

"Yep," Warden said. "Just like you read in the report."

SEVEN

GUSTAVE WARDEN GAVE ME general directions to Great Bay. It turned out to be a thirty-minute drive from Coram. On the way I enjoyed my first real feeling of progress. Warden had been exactly what I'd needed. Talking to him had reminded me of listening to my grandfather's stories when I was young. I'd had the same feeling of the proximity of the past and of continuity. The grease on Warden's hands was only the latest in an unbroken stream that led back to the Warner radial of the *Phaeton*. The thought made me smile. Just learning the name of Carteret's plane had made my trip to Long Island a success.

I hadn't thought to look up Carteret's address, and the size of Great Bay surprised me. The second filling station I tried sent me out of the town proper, toward the south-east. I drove past a mile or two of New York's new bedrooms. The developments had names like Churchill Acres and Thornebrook, names that confirmed that they were the descendants of Brooklyn's aristocratic apartment buildings. The houses I passed were large, but fairly similar, and the properties they occupied were small.

The green iron fence of the Carteret estate began a few feet past the last mock Tudor. No more than a couple of seconds worth of green fence had swept by me before I came to an entrance. It was small and unmarked. On either side of a narrow drive, low brick walls connected the green fence to matching green gates. A stainless steel intercom was set in one of the walls. I pulled up beside it and stopped.

I wasn't sure if I'd found the main entrance or a service road. Through the gates and a stand of old pines I could see the brick wall of a house and a French window. I pressed the intercom's single button and waited. The conversation that followed was extremely polite.

"May I help you?" a voice from the speaker asked.

"I would like to see Mr. Carteret," I said.

"Please don't press the button to speak. It only rings the bell."

"Sorry."

"Please state your name and your business with Mr. Carteret."

"My name is Owen Keane. I work for a law firm engaged by Mr. Carteret to look into a confidential matter."

"I'm sorry. Mr. Carteret is unavailable at the present time."

"Would it be possible to make an appointment to see him?"

"All inquiries of that nature should be directed to the Carteret Corporation. I can give you a name."

"Thank you."

"Please contact John Hyatt at the Carteret Federal Building."

"Thanks. I have one more question. Does Mr. Carteret employ someone here at the house named Gregson?"

"Mr. Hyatt can probably answer that for you."

"Thanks a lot." For practically nothing.

After returning the car to Tommy (there were thirty-nine stones in the Beryl Coronet), I walked to the Carteret Federal Building at Fifty-fifth and Madison.

The building was a brick dwarf in the glass and steel banking district. I guessed that it had been built in the thirties, from the art deco influence that showed itself in vertical lines of yellow tile running through the staid brown brick. It was a good thirty stories, and the topmost third was stepped, like a wedding cake. An octagonal tower made up the last five stories. Carolyn Vernia's aerie, I thought. As I approached, I saw that the specific motif of the building was Egyptian. Stylized slaves decorated the bronze screen that framed the main entrance. The dark green stone of the lobby was inset with bronze hieroglyphics.

The building pleased me in the same way Gus Warden had, by satisfying my anticipation and by providing a tangible link with my intangible problem, William Carteret. I felt I was walking in his footsteps as I crossed the lobby.

A young woman at a semicircular stone desk asked if Mr. Hyatt was expecting me.

"I wouldn't be a bit surprised," I said.

The automatic elevator announced my arrival on the fifth floor with a gonglike bell. Hyatt's secretary looked disappointed when I walked in. I decided that she had been expecting someone else, and I thought briefly of apologizing. Her reception area was larger than Hyatt's office. The man himself was short and a little overweight, but he had a firm handshake.

"How are you? Have a seat," Hyatt said. "I'm not familiar with your firm, do you do much business with us?"

"Only odd jobs," I said.

"Your position is?"

"Researcher."

"That sounds like a euphemism."

"Like public relations?" I asked.

"Yes. More like a collective in our case. We wear a lot of hats."

I wanted to say, "and I wear out a lot of shoes," but our tone was already too familiar for me. I smiled instead.

"Have you studied law?" Hyatt asked.

"No. Everything else."

"That's the way it seems to work out." He was smiling, too. "I was an English major, myself. My banking career grew out of a summer job. I should really be teaching Keats somewhere. 'Beauty is truth, truth beauty.'"

"'That is all ye know on earth, and all ye need to know,'" I said in reply. Circular Keats given as sign and countersign, I hoped. Hyatt considered me more carefully for a moment before looking down at a paper on his desk.

"I believe you inquired about a Mr. Gregson," he said.

"Only as a second choice. I really wanted to speak with Mr. Carteret."

He nodded to the paper conspiratorially. "You mentioned a commission from Mr. Carteret."

"Yes."

"Could you expand on that?"

"Not very much, I'm afraid. Discretion was the primary requirement. I can say that it involves a family incident that occurred quite some time ago. Our communication with Mr. Carteret has been con-

ducted through your legal department. They can ver-
ify our relationship."

I watched him closely during my speech to see if my
businesslike delivery had convinced him. Instead, he
looked confused, and I remembered that the shirt I
wore had a frayed collar.

"I see," he said without conviction. "You wish to
make a report to Mr. Carteret."

"Actually, we've only just begun our research.
What I was really hoping for was clarification of several points and possibly some redirection."

"I won't pretend to understand, since the business
is so confidential," Hyatt said, "but I'll see what I can
do. Maybe Legal can help me." He punched four digits
into the phone at his elbow. "Mr. Bonsett, please.
Okay. Hello, Sue. Is Larry in? Never mind, I'll come
up. Thanks." Hyatt returned to his introductory smile.
"Would you excuse me for a moment, Mr. Keane? I
won't be long."

In fact, he was almost half an hour. After ten minutes, Hyatt's secretary brought me a cup of coffee and
told me she was going on break, which left me alone
in the office. I began to feel a growing inclination to
panic, to take the first elevator down and to keep going. In a compromise decision, I rose and walked to
Hyatt's single window. The late afternoon traffic was
picking up.

Unexpectedly, I began to think of Marilyn and to
wonder, too late, if my current bluster was the result
of her "fantasy world" remark. I felt trapped in the
unguarded office by my own half-thought-out actions.

In that quiet moment by the window, I remembered the feelings of a morning of my fifth year. Jeal-

ous of my older brother's homework assignments, I
had invented one of my own. I had then somehow
convinced my mother that her son, who barely knew
his letters, had been instructed to write an essay. At the
table after dinner, standing with my chin as high as her
moving pen, I'd dictated my views on Catholic edu-
cation. My undoing came the next day, when I
couldn't read my masterpiece before the audience of
nuns my baffled teacher had assembled. Beware false
prodigy.

The embarrassment of that early failure to sub-
stantiate my pretense came again and left me quickly
as I stood in Hyatt's office. I walked tentatively out to
the reception area. It occurred to me that the elevator
Hyatt must have taken betrayed its comings with a
loud bell. The hallway seemed an untraveled back-
water and the secretary would be gone for another ten
minutes. I decided that it was better to be hung as an
amateur detective than as a delinquent researcher.

The filing cabinets that lined the wall opposite the
secretary's desk were unlocked. After checking the hall
quickly, I dug into the C's. I flipped through two
drawers of Carteret businesses before I found Robert's folder. It was marked with his name and 1981.
Inside were some programs and handbills for the Great
Bay horse show and other deductible activities of the
same type. There was also a piece of plain white bond
on which was typed, word for word, the brief biographical sketch I'd found in the library the day before. The chief executive officer didn't generate much
publicity.

I returned the folder and moved down the row for a
look at Carolyn Vernia. Her folder was several times
the thickness of Carteret's. A photograph was paper

clipped to the inside cover. In its annual report pose, she sat in a leather wing chair with her hands folded in her lap. Either it was an unusually large chair, or she was a small person. I also couldn't decide whether she was really as old as the boxy style of her brown hair made her look. She had a pleasant smile and large, direct brown eyes.

At that moment the elevator bell sounded. I froze foolishly for an instant. Then I returned the folder and crossed, with an awkward attempt at noiselessness, to Hyatt's office. I sat with equally awkward nonchalance, almost laughing at my own stiffness but unable to relax.

When Hyatt entered, he was smiling, too, and I had the uncomfortable feeling that he was sharing my joke.

"Sorry to have kept you waiting," he said. "Jill desert you?"

"Break." I didn't trust myself with a long answer.

"Oh." Hyatt seemed distracted for a moment, as though the length of Jill's breaks was more important than our business. Then he sat down, smiled slightly, and began. "Lawrence Bonsett in Legal confirmed your assignment. He was of the opinion, however, that the original instructions were sufficient. He did suggest that you might submit any questions you have with the first draft of your report. Mr. Carteret could address those areas and request additional information as he saw fit. I'm afraid that's the best I can do for you at the moment."

"I appreciate your help," I said, greatly relieved. "Could you answer a quick question for me yourself?" Hyatt looked doubtful. "I'll try," he said.

"What's Mr. Carteret like?"

"I wouldn't be much of a public relations man, Mr. Keane, if I went around giving my opinion of the boss. As it happens, I can evade that question easily enough. I've never met Mr. Carteret. The few dealings I've had with the estate have been handled by Mr. Carteret's private secretary, Ms. Pritchard. She spoke with me today about your visit."

"Was she able to give you any information on Mr. Gregson?"

"Yes, as a matter of fact." Hyatt searched his desktop briefly for his notes. "He was the Carteret grounds keeper until he retired in 1958. He continued to live on the estate until 1963, when he passed away."

We shook hands as we parted, but I felt uneasy until I'd passed through the Egyptian gates. Then, being jostled by the sidewalk traffic in the crisp air made me think I'd exaggerated my risk and underestimated my ability. Hyatt's basic message had been a dismissal, but it had been civilized enough. Of course, it had also been too simple a reply to account for the length of time he'd been gone from the office. But that didn't suggest to me that I was being set up. Or that I would step into the trap at the offices of Ohlman, Ohlman, and Pulsifer.

Harry was back from Boston and waiting to see me.

EIGHT

THE GRAY TWILIGHT HAD a pleasant bluish tint through the windows of Harry's darkened office. In the blue light I could see that he was seated behind his desk. He was wearing his suit coat, which was out of character. His opening remarks surprised me even more.

"You're still a pain in the ass, Owen," he said. "When we were all in school, Mary used to say that you were a faux waiting to pas. I knew even then you were just a pain in the ass."

I sat down heavily. More than his words, Harry's tone told me that a pretense more important to me than the one I'd acted out with Hyatt was in danger.

"If we're going to talk old times," I said, "let's have that drink you promised me."

It was his turn to look surprised, but only, I think, because he hadn't thought of it himself. He pointed to a cabinet to my left. "There's no ice," he said.

I brought a bottle of scotch and two glasses back to the desk and poured the first round. It seemed the appropriate drink, given Harry's nostalgic mood. He and I had taught ourselves to like scotch when we were freshmen together.

"Back in the old days," I said, "I thought you were a plain ass."

Harry turned away from me toward the window. "Do you think I deserved that?" he asked, sounding ridiculously proper.

"I don't know, Harry. I figured you were trying to fire me and I thought I'd help you along."

"Jesus Christ, Owen."

"I thought you were an ass then, Harry, but I don't anymore. You grew up. I didn't."

"You have though," Harry said. "You've grown into a full-time problem. If you don't want to work for me, why don't you just quit?"

I was tempted to do just that, to remove the responsibility for me from Harry's unwilling shoulders. I was tempted, but I had nowhere else to go. "You just get back?" I asked.

"Yes," Harry's silhouette replied. "I saw the old campus while I was there. They're still changing the place. They've finished the new theater building. Built it right in the middle of the old 'dust bowl.' I really hated to lose that quad. It always reminded me of the day you were arrested."

"Have you commissioned a plaque?"

"Not yet. My sensitive side, Mary, tells me never to mention that business in front of you, but I'm feeling insensitive this evening." And, as I had observed, nostalgic. "Do you remember the time I found you crying by the reservoir?" Harry asked. "I turned the whole campus upside down that night."

"Saved my life," I said.

"I didn't think things through in those days. Didn't think very well, generally speaking. For example, I thought you were a cross between Charlie Chan and Mahatma Gandhi. I couldn't distinguish between inscrutable and incoherent."

"The disease of age, Harry. Is there a point to any of this?"

"I don't know," Harry said. "Certainly not in your celestial scheme of things." He stretched across an arm's length of walnut to refill my glass. "As you've probably deduced by now, I received a call a short time ago from the Carteret Corporation. The head of their legal department again. I'd tell you the man's name but you'd be interviewing his wife tomorrow morning."

"Lawrence Bonsett," I said.

"Yes, of course. Elementary. Mr. Bonsett wanted to tell me how diligent one of our people had been."

The room was too dark now. I leaned forward and switched on a small brass desk lamp which was largely ornamental. It lit the center of the desk without showing me more of Harry than the color of his tie. "I would have told you all about it tomorrow, Harry."

"As an act of contrition. Telling me about it yesterday would have flattered me greatly."

"I'm sorry."

"It was difficult for me to explain to Mr. Bonsett how the man I'd sent to the New York Public Library could turn up on Long Island."

"You told him that we were conducting the research and that we would organize it as we saw fit within the boundaries of discretion."

"No. I didn't. I also didn't say, 'Forgive me, Mr. Bonsett, the offending individual will be shelving books in Perth Amboy tomorrow.' Either of those would have been excellent replies, had I thought to make one of them. Instead, I wandered around an embarrassing middle ground of mild shock."

"Are you mad at me for exceeding my authority or for making you look silly?"

"I'm still mad at you for the first time you made me look silly, fourteen years ago, and the odd hundred times since. That's beside the point."

Harry reached into a drawer and produced a pack of cigarettes. I saw his face clearly for a second in the light of the match. He looked tired.

"Sorry again," I said.

"Forget it," he said, misinterpreting my apology. "I cheated on the plane anyway." He smoked half of the cigarette quickly and in silence. "Your instructions weren't so explicit that you couldn't move around a bit," he said, finally. "It was the direction you decided to take. Robert Carteret, for God's sake. I don't even mind you trying to pass yourself off as Paul Drake, the television private eye. But I told you that Carteret chose to be inaccessible. I may not know as much as my father about handling monied nuts, but I know enough not to act directly against their wishes."

"Robert Carteret is not a 'monied nut,'" I said.

"Is that based on information or insight?"

"My latest hunch." I stirred myself in my chair. I'd started to slump during Harry's reprimand and that unconscious reaction irritated me. "If you're done working yourself up, I'd like to use the towel for a while. Not only weren't my instructions explicit, they were intentionally vague and deceptive."

"You'd better explain that."

"Let's start with our basic premise. Robert Carteret decides that he wants to know about his brother's death. He wants to find out all about it. The only knowledge he reveals in his letter of instruction is the date his brother died. He doesn't ask specific questions or request that specific areas be explored. He's just curious. That's a little odd, don't you think?"

"Yes," Harry said.

"At the moment I see two possible explanations. The first is that he really doesn't know a thing about his brother's death. He's been so busy setting up horse shows that he's never looked into it. Does that sound reasonable to you, Harry?"

"No."

"The second explanation is that he knows all about his brother's death, or at least as much as he cares to know. He's really requesting that we find out how much a curious person could learn about the crash after forty years. In other words, are there any tracks left to cover? That's the explanation that appeals to me at the moment."

"Okay. I can see how you might consider his instructions deceptive."

"His and yours both, Harry. Don't let me off the hook so easily. You sent me out of here with a letter of instruction you knew was a ringer." My irritation carried me away. "When I tried to make a serious job of it, people who shouldn't even give a damn came up swinging."

"I see," Harry said. "This is the point in the story when a bomb tossed through the window convinces the detective he's onto something." Sometimes Harry sounded so much like Marilyn that I found it hard to remember they'd never met.

"Meaning what?" I asked.

"Meaning that I don't mind your representing yourself as a detective, as long as you don't start believing you are one. Or start seeing plots."

"You didn't tell me you knew about Robert Carteret." I was tired, too. I'd had too much running around that day and too much of the nervous excitement that came from dealing with people instead of books. The scotch and the soft chair were working together to make me feel disinterested and detached when I should have been alert. "I'm referring to the confidential job your father did for the Carteret Corporation. I'm supposed to believe that it was so confidential he forgot it himself. I don't know Harold Ohlman, Sr., very well, but I don't think he's forgotten a case or a piece of gossip since he stepped off the train from Boston."

"We decided that it didn't have any bearing on this inquiry."

"'We decided'? So you did know about it."

"You're making too much of it, Owen. My father believes in discretion. To him, being discreet doesn't mean discussing a client's affairs with selected people. It means discussing them with no one. If it makes you feel any better, he wouldn't even tell me about it over the phone. I had no idea what we'd done for Robert Carteret when I gave you the assignment, believe it or not."

"I believe you," I said.

"I met with Dad yesterday about the Boston trip."

"And you asked him."

"Yes."

"And?"

"We annulled his marriage." Even in the semi-darkness my face must have conveyed my reaction. "Incredulity suits you, Owen. Robert Carteret married in 1951. He was married for a day. Dad was engaged to do the paperwork on the annulment."

"Who did he marry?"

"Whom. His nurse. He was convalescing at the time, or rather, he was supposed to be. How's your drink?"

"And he arranged for the annulment?"

"No. Carl Vernia was running his errands at that point. I told you about him."

"What were the grounds?"

"When did this reprimand become a cross-examination? The grounds were medical and academic."

"I don't understand."

"He was supposedly on some medication at the time. But the grounds were just a technicality, like the paperwork. Everything was rubber stamped under the table, to compound my clichés. In any case, it has no bearing on the death of William Carteret in 1941."

I felt much more awake now. "Anything that reveals Robert Carteret in any way has bearing," I said. "You haven't asked me what I've found after two days of research. That's okay, because I've found very little. Very little press on the disappearance of two people and a plane. Very little curiosity in the inquiry into their deaths. Very little trace of the surviving brother. What I did uncover wasn't encouraging. More motive for Robert Carteret to do away with his brother than we already had, and opportunity. I am seeing plots, Harry. Or traces of old plots."

"Why would Carteret suddenly be worried about covering his tracks, assuming there are tracks?"

"I don't know. I guess that's what I wanted to ask him."

Harry blew a long stream of smoke toward the dark ceiling. "Now I'm almost sorry you didn't get in." He stood slowly and walked away from me and the small circle of light.

"Have we been dismissed?" I asked.

"No." Harry was standing by the window, looking out at the city. "Bonsett doesn't carry that kind of weight."

"He would if Carteret were unhappy with my work."

"I see your point, I think."

I took a swallow of scotch. "Do I still have a job?"

Harry returned to his chair. "Owen," he said. "Yes. I'm going to have a hard enough time explaining the drinking without further incurring Mary's wrath. She's still very fond of you, but that's something else I'm not supposed to talk about."

"Am I still on the Carteret project?"

"I note, thankfully, that you didn't say 'case.' Yes, you're still on the project, provided you promise to advise me of any field trips in advance."

"Agreed. Do you have any contacts in Albany?"

"The fiancée?"

"Her name was Lynn Baxter. I'd like to talk with her family if there are any left."

"What do you expect to find?"

"Breathing bodies would be nice. Someone has the archives buttoned up tight. I have to fall back on the gossip."

"Write down the particulars. I've a favor or two I can call in."

"Thanks."

"You'll want to fly up there, I suppose."

"Carteret can afford it."

"Anything else?"

"I'll need the name of Carteret's one-day wife."

"I suppose I should be surprised, but I'm not. Her maiden name was Mildred Fell. Her married name is Tucker."

"How do you happen to know she remarried?" I asked.

"The scotch must be slowing your deductive powers. It seems that our firm manages a trust fund that produces a monthly check for Mrs. Tucker. A by-product of the annulment. That innocent-looking loose end was easy to find in our files."

"Good work."

"Call me Watson and I'll fire you yet."

WE FINISHED MOST of Harry's scotch that night, each for reasons of our own. Even though he became sentimental toward the end and our professional relationship regained its equilibrium, I sensed that things had changed for Harry and me. I don't really mean that our relationship had changed; the basic truth of it couldn't change. Rather, a single layer of the pretense that made that truth harder to see and understand, and possibly easier to live with, had been taken away. Harry and I didn't have many layers left.

In contrast, Robert Carteret stood at the center of the earth.

NINE

HARRY AND I HELD our little drinking party on a Friday night. On the following Monday morning, I flew to Albany. Harry's contacts had worked quickly and mysteriously and had produced the name and address of Lynn Baxter's sister. Harry didn't tell me if they'd hired a real detective, someone who would meet me at the Albany County Airport in a rumpled suit and sprinkle cigar ashes on my false confidence. I knew they hadn't just looked in the phone book; the sister was married. I didn't know how I would have found her myself. I might have asked Marilyn.

Ms. Kiefner had booked my flight with a lesser-known airline. It claimed to be one of the larger domestic carriers on the basis of cities served, but that was only, I think, because their planes were too small for extended flights. My plane was a tiny jet stopping briefly in Albany on its way west. Our stewardess was a little bit of New York City we carried north with us. She was small and attractive and vaguely Italian and reminded me of Marilyn. That is, she reminded me of her until she moved. Then she looked like Marilyn played at seventy-eight instead of thirty-three. Her animation suggested New York City to me more distinctly than her polished Bronx. She didn't simply recite the seat belt instructions, she performed them. Her spirited rendition of the oxygen mask procedure actually won a hand.

There was something of the would-be actress about her, or rather the actress who happened at the moment to be working as a stewardess, that also reminded me of our mutual city. New York sometimes seemed to me to be a place where a dreamer needed only the credentials of self-belief to be accepted, at least by the other dreamers. The sort of mental aberrations that set people apart in small towns made them come to New York to find in some mutual sympathy the credibility that sustains serious dreaming.

I smiled in my small airliner's small seat at that romantic view of New York, because of the eloquent grimace I knew it would have produced from Marilyn. She seemed to be in every other thought for me that morning.

I'd spent an empty, nervous weekend waiting for Mildred Tucker to answer her phone or for some word to come from Albany. I'd also tried to call Marilyn, without success. I had some idea that my little victory over Harry would work as a peace offering, or as an opening line for the conversation we'd never had. In any case, she didn't answer. She and Mildred may have been walking the beach together, discussing how best to handle my next move. A lot of what I could remember from those two days was the frustrating ritual of dialing and counting the rings.

The sunlight above the clouds was the first I'd seen in several days. As we climbed, the cloud layer became the vague landscape of a frozen and forbidding world. The idea that I was re-creating William Carteret's announced flight plan wasn't lost on me in my melancholy mood. I might have flown south at that moment myself, given the chance.

I sipped my courtesy soda with the caution of an infrequent flier and thought again of Marilyn. Throughout my lonely weekend, I'd put off thinking about my last evening with her and about her angry reaction to the Carteret story. Her anger was another mystery, and I already had more of those than I could handle. But now, as the airliner droned on, I replayed the fatal conversation, looking for the trip wire I'd somehow strung for myself. The exercise was depressing and futile. I began instead rerunning highlights from our early relationship, searching for clues.

MY FIRST EVENING OUT with Marilyn had more than the usual amount of groping awkwardness. I overproduced it, not knowing that her tastes ran toward simpler, less public evenings. Dinner was compromised by a difficult waiter, and the play I'd selected contained in its title and every other line a word Marilyn thought little of: *romance*. Fortunately for me, the play also had a cast of big names led by a famous English actor. He distracted Marilyn somewhat, but she shifted restlessly when he was offstage and sniffed pointedly at selected lines.

At intermission we had a drink in the theater's small lounge that overlooked Times Square. Marilyn talked a little about her career over dinner. She had fallen into graduate school and library science when her undergraduate degree had proven unnegotiable. Later, she'd discovered that she actually liked the work, that she enjoyed being a "finder of facts." My misinterpretation of this led to our first "discussion."

Over our drinks, I volunteered a story from my distant past concerning a teenager named Jimmy whom I'd met at a summer retreat. It wasn't a story I told often or easily. I trotted it out for Marilyn, a relative stranger, because her finder-of-facts remark had reminded me of it and had made me think that she might be a kindred soul. Jimmy had a claim to fame that had made him stand out in that long-ago gathering of high school students. It would have distinguished him in any group, in fact, and in any age. He told us that he had been spoken to by God.

I had successfully solved a small mystery related to Jimmy's story, and that early triumph had fooled me into believing that I could solve anything, even the unanswerable question at the heart of Jimmy's claim. At the time I resurrected Jimmy for Marilyn, I had been forced by years of failure to reassess my abilities as an investigator. Still, I held the old tale out to Marilyn that night as evidence that once I had been, if not a finder of facts, at least a searcher. I failed to anticipate how critical that distinction would be to Marilyn.

"You really thought you could track down God?" Marilyn asked me. "What, with a fingerprint kit and a magnifying glass?"

"Something like that," I admitted.

"What were you smoking in those days?"

I'd asked myself that same question, or variations of it, often enough, but hearing it from Marilyn that evening embarrassed and hurt me. I struggled on briefly in defense of my past self. "I saw people back then as clues to a big mystery," I told her. "As clues to God, to life, whatever. I thought that if I could just figure out the little mysteries, and collect enough of the little answers, I might solve the big mystery."

Marilyn was polite enough to tone down her smile. "So what happened?" she asked.

"I stopped finding the little answers. After a while, I stopped looking. I ended up in a library, writing down names and dates."

The lights in the lounge blinked off and on, warning us of the start of the next act. Marilyn didn't stir. "Those names and dates are the answer, Keane," she said. "Those are the facts. That's all there is. You can't know any more. You'll only make yourself crazy if you try to."

I'd had enough exposure for one evening, so I held my peace. I'd already revealed enough to spoil the evening and to make Marilyn wary of me for weeks.

After a period of penance, during which I toiled diligently in her library after simple, garden-variety facts, Marilyn gave me another chance. This time she planned the evening, and it set the pattern for most of our subsequent "dates." We spent it in bed.

Afterward, as we sat among the covers eating the breakfast cereal that Marilyn called dinner, she returned to the subject of our talk in the theater lounge. "I shouldn't have laughed at your story about Jimmy, Keane," she said.

I told her not to apologize.

"I'm not apologizing," Marilyn said. "You can tell when I'm apologizing because all my hair stands on end."

I brushed a heavy lock from her forehead. "I understand," I said.

"I just wanted to tell you that I've thought about it and decided that I was pretty stupid. If you'd told me that you'd had a drinking problem, I wouldn't have made drunk jokes. I would have congratulated you for getting straight. I would have supported you." She put her hand on my arm. "I am supporting you," she said.

I found Marilyn's nonapology almost as hard to take as her earlier laughter. It reminded me of a feeling I'd often had at Ohlman, Ohlman, and Pulsifer, the feeling that I was being rehabilitated. But Marilyn's hand on my arm and her offer of support iced my bruised ego. We ended the discussion in a clinch suitable for a Hollywood fadeout.

That evening really began what I've already described as our intermittent but improving relationship. At least it had been improving, until the Carteret brothers showed up.

THE STEWARDESS CAME BY with a plastic shopping bag and claimed my empty cup. The engines changed their tone, and, to my left, my frozen landscape was rising to meet us. I took a last sentimental look at the sunlight and closed my eyes.

Immediately, I began again reliving the last time I'd spent with Marilyn, when she'd suddenly frosted over and mysteriously warned me off the Carteret case. I still didn't want to think about that night, but the episode now fit chronologically in my little retrospective of our affair. All at once, it fit in other ways, too. Remembering Marilyn's drinking-problem analogy turned the key. I realized that she saw the Carteret mystery as a potential relapse. She thought I was in danger of falling off the sanity wagon.

I had been slow to recognize her concern because I'd never thought of myself as someone who needed rehabilitating. I saw Owen Keane as a failure, yes, but not as a reformed lunatic. I was secretly afraid that I would fail again with the Carterets. Marilyn, I now saw, was afraid that I would succeed.

TEN

No DETECTIVE MET ME at the airport, so I followed my sketchy plan and rented a car. The sister's name was Lois Parnell, and she was married to a teacher at Albany State College. That, and their address, was all the information Harry could give me. I'd taken the obvious precaution of phoning the woman from the office to find out if she would even allow a visit. She'd agreed to see me, but she'd been terse and hesitant and our conversation had been brief.

I followed the rental agent's instructions and drove west from the airport. As I drove I tried, unsuccessfully, to rediscover the bluster that had carried me so close to the brink with Harry. I'd asked the rental agent about Westpark, the exclusive-sounding address of the Baxters, and she'd told me that it wasn't much of a neighborhood anymore. It had been compromised by a giant shopping mall. I thought of that mall during my drive, and it reminded me of the minimansions encroaching on the Carteret estate. I wondered why that encroachment didn't bother Robert Carteret as much as it bothered me.

Albany State College was easy to find, although it was small. It was also fairly new, and it showed its youth in unflattering ways, as the Great Bay subdivisions had, with half-grown trees and economy architecture.

The Parnells lived a block or so from the abrupt meeting of the campus and the suburbs. Their home was a Dutch colonial with a fieldstone chimney and paint that predated the college. It had established trees around it and shrubs and ground cover that were fighting each other for room. Somehow the overall effect was not of neglect. The yard reminded me of the cultivated wilds of a more romantic England, reflecting a sensitivity to nature rather than an insensitivity to neighbors. On the side of the house nearest the road there was a glassed-in porch. Within it I could see crammed, irregular bookshelves. In the corners, piles of books had grown as high as the light of the windows. I left my car feeling that my escape from the library had been an illusion.

I rang the bell and listened to the sound of a dog charging from the depths of the house. I judged it to be a large dog by the bass tone of its bark, and I deduced, from its scratching and sliding approach, that the house had hardwood floors. When the door opened to the length of its security chain, the black muzzle of a Labrador protruded. Above it a thin and pale woman's face spoke through the storm door. "Mr. Keane?" she asked.

I nodded, and the black muzzle was dragged backward, protesting. I gathered from the orders being issued that the dog's name was Basil. Mrs. Parnell opened the storm door and smiled. "I'm sorry about that reception," she said.

I gave her my card, which she ignored, and my overcoat, which she carried into the next room. The dog followed her and considered me darkly from the doorway. Mrs. Parnell pushed him aside with her leg on her return trip.

"It will take Basil a little time to get used to you," she said.

The feeling was mutual. "I appreciate your making time to see me," I said. "I hope this isn't too unpleasant for you."

She smiled at that. She had a pleasant face, with the same large eyes I'd noted in her sister's picture. Her blond hair was drawn back tightly and gathered in a bun. The result was more pleasant than severe, a practical example of the long-term advantages of good bones. She was slender, a fact conveyed in an understated way by her loose sweater and corduroys. Lynn Baxter at fifty-five.

"My sister has been gone for forty years," she said. "I'm more curious about your visit than anything else. Won't you sit down?"

She chose a sofa cluttered with magazines and papers, the leitmotif of the room. I sat opposite her in an armchair I suspected had been cleared for the occasion. There was a black-on-white print on the wall to my left, featuring tribal warriors with randomly disproportionate limbs. On my right a small table held the ubiquitous papers and a plaster head. The head was dark gray and surfaced with tiny peaks as though it had been drawn wet from a mold. The face, which was dominated by a large nose, held an expression of frozen surprise.

"My husband." Mrs. Parnell had followed my gaze. "One of his students did that of him and he took a liking to it." Her tone added the "unfortunately."

"Does he teach art?" I asked.

"No," she said, still examining the bust, "psychology. However, the facial expression would apply equally well to any academic discipline. Would you like any coffee? Sherry? Well then, perhaps you can tell me how my sister comes to interest you. You mentioned the Carteret family on the phone."

"Yes. Robert Carteret has engaged us to compile a report on the death of his brother, William." Unlike Harold Ohlman, Sr., I could be as casual with my discretion as I chose to be.

Mrs. Parnell looked disappointed. "I'm afraid I can tell you very little about the way William Carteret died, except that he died with my sister, which you obviously already know. I always thought that Carteret and Lynn were an unlikely couple. William Carteret, I mean. Nothing but the fact of their death together enables me to link them at all, really. I never knew many of the details of the accident. I was only fifteen at the time and my mother didn't speak of it often."

"Did she have any idea why they were flying south?"

"That especially was not spoken of."

"I'm sorry."

"Please, Mr. Keane, don't apologize. I was speaking of my mother's sensitivity, not my own. She's been gone now for twenty years, my father for ten. I've been to college, married, and raised my own family since Lynn's death. I never knew many of the details of the accident, as I've said, and I'm afraid I've also forgotten most of the feelings of that time."

The black muzzle appeared around the corner of my chair, sniffing at my ankles. It worked its way up to my lap, and I was embarrassed into crossing my legs and leaning back informally.

"We raised Labradors for a time," Mrs. Parnell said. "Basil is the only one left. He wasn't suitable for show, his tail's too short, but he's good around people.'' I already knew that Basil would rather drool than bark, which is all ''good around people'' usually meant.

''Did you think Robert Carteret and your sister were a better couple?'' I asked.

''Yes, as a matter of fact I did. Did Robert instruct you to ask me that?''

''My instructions from Robert Carteret were as simple as I've described them.'' I pulled my briefcase from between the chair and the dog. ''All I know of Robert and your sister comes from this.'' I laid the photocopy of her sister's presentation story on the coffee table between us.

She held it up to catch the light from the windows behind her, blocking her face from my view. ''Yes,'' she said. ''Robert was a good deal less worldly than his brother. Less spoiled by it all. I'm not trying to speak against William. What you've asked me for are the impressions made on a fifteen-year-old mind. It just seemed to me that Lynn disappeared in William's presence, became part of the background. Rather like a Hollywood extra. You're more likely to notice Clark Gable's tie than the person standing next to him in a crowd.''

''I thought your sister was an attractive woman.''

She liked that for some reason. ''Yes, she was beautiful. But it wasn't a flashy, room-filling beauty. Robert Carteret was a handsome young man, for that matter. Their quieter styles, hers understated and his, I think, inexperienced, complemented each other.''

Mrs. Parnell leaned forward to retrieve a white box from beneath the coffee table. Basil misinterpreted the movement and walked over to be petted. The box contained photographs.

"You might be interested in this," she said, handing me a large print. It was of Lynn and William Carteret. They were sitting at a table set with empty plates and beer bottles. Lynn wore a pullover sweater like her sister. Her hair was wound in elaborate coils on either side of her head. That and the thinness of her face made her look younger than my newspaper photographs.

"That was taken almost two years before her death," Mrs. Parnell said.

"She looks so young," I said, as though I was used to seeing some older version.

That odd comment matched a thought for Mrs. Parnell. "She was always young. I used to think sometimes that she wasn't much older than I."

I handed the photograph back. "Have you any of Robert Carteret?" I asked.

She turned the picture over and held it out for me to take again. On the back was written "Lynn and Robert Carteret, Daley Hall, June, 1939."

"I thought you'd be interested in that photo because it's the only one I have of Robert. Mother once told me that Lynn had thrown the rest of them away."

"I thought it was William," I said. "There's quite a family resemblance."

"You wouldn't have thought that if you'd known them." She handed me another photograph, this one of a Carteret standing next to a woman wearing a broad hat. "That's William with my mother."

I held the photographs side by side and saw that the two were just brothers after all and not twins. Their features were similar, but Robert was thinner and a little darker. He also seemed listless in comparison to William, whose suit looked a half size too small.

"Robert was quite an admirer of his brother," Mrs. Parnell said, "like most of William's world. I think Robert heightened their resemblance by imitating him, consciously or unconsciously. It wasn't a very good imitation, except perhaps on the surface."

"You said most of William's world admired him. Who didn't?"

"You've caught me on an unsupported statement, Mr. Keane. At fifteen I wasn't privy to my elders' opinions. I certainly didn't know much of William Carteret's world. But I did have the feeling that my parents were wary of William, thought him too much for Lynn to handle. When the accident occurred I think they felt, or at least my mother felt, that it was a direct result of a star-crossed combination, and not just an accident.

"I'm afraid the Baxters were social climbers. My father was only a moderately successful businessman, but his family had roots in this state that were fairly well established. We even had a Civil War hero, I think, but nothing else dramatic to recommend us. Except for my mother's ambition, of course. She saw William as a brilliant catch, and naturally he was, but I think that even she felt he was out of our league."

"I get the impression that you didn't admire William yourself."

"True, but I think it was less a lack of feeling for William than too much feeling for Robert. I found it hard not to blame William for Robert and my sister breaking up. I suppose I had a crush on Robert."

"How were the two of them different?"

She examined the top of Basil's broad head for a moment. "It was a difference in sensitivity, really. Without being too hard on William, I don't think he was a very sensitive man. Do you like old movies, Mr. Keane?"

"Some."

"Well, at the time I thought of Robert as Leslie Howard or Ronald Colman."

"And William as Clark Gable?"

"Or Errol Flynn." She smiled. "Not a bad man, but not an examining man either. Maybe that was their basic difference. One was sensitive to the world around him. The other countered the world with a strong projection of himself."

"It seems like that combination in brothers would be hard on the receptive one," I said.

"I think the effect would be mainly superficial, as I said before. That's what a personality like William's projects: superficialities. The flying and the clothes and the Carteret smile were as much as he could inflict on Robert. It was enough to give a casual observer the impression that Robert had disappeared, but that wasn't the case. He was stronger than William, even if he didn't realize it himself. Herman Melville nothwithstanding, I think it's much harder to receive the world on its own terms than to project your presence on a tiny corner. Any fool with a microphone can do that, as we've all learned." She shook her head. "I'm afraid I'm rambling," she said.

I silently hoped that Professor Parnell took notes when his wife was rambling. "Your sister didn't recognize the distinction," I said.

"She was very young. My views have been tempered by forty years in the world. And William was an attractive man. It was Robert's own fault that he lost her, although lost may not be the right word. They were only serious for a summer or so. I mean that

Lynn can hardly be blamed for falling for the real
William Carteret when Robert offered a pale imitation and nothing of himself.

"Lynn was visiting the Carteret home on Long Island when she met William. I think Robert wanted her
to meet his father. William started flying up to Albany on weekends shortly after that."

"Lynn started seeing William while Charles Carteret was still alive?"

"Yes." If Mrs. Parnell understood my question, she
didn't let it show.

"How did Robert take it?"

"I don't know, but I would guess he took it badly.
He disappeared about that time, as far as I was concerned. I wasn't encouraged to speak of him."

"You mentioned earlier that your mother didn't
think the crash was an accident."

"I only meant that she thought it was some sort of
retribution or punishment for her family ambitions.
She took Lynn's death very, very hard."

"Do you think the crash was an accident?"

"I have no reason to think it was not."

"Was the possibility that the plane had been tampered with ever discussed?"

"Not in front of me."

"Do you think Robert was capable of that kind of
action?"

"Not against Lynn. I can't imagine him doing anything that might hurt her." She seemed irritated by the
suggestion. "I thought you represented Robert Carteret," she said.

"I do, in a manner of speaking."

"You don't seem particularly interested in protecting his reputation."

"He didn't hire me to protect anything. I'm trying to find out what happened to his brother on a day in 1941."

"No other motivation?"

"None that straightforward."

Mrs. Parnell looked down at the coffee table. "Lynn is buried in the Presbyterian cemetery a few miles from here," she said.

That leap left me behind for a second. The only connection I could think of was an odd one. "Speaking of old movies," I said, "did you like *Laura*?"

"Yes," Mrs. Parnell said, "I was a big fan of Dana Andrews."

"And I like Gene Tierney, but I thought the plot was a little improbable."

"Hard-boiled detectives don't fall in love with dead girls' pictures?"

"I can only speak for the three-minute variety."

She wasn't sold. Her older, younger sister was still a romantic figure to her, someone men fell in love with.

"May I borrow these photographs long enough to have them copied?" I asked.

"Yes," she said, "if you promise to call me someday and tell me what you found out about Lynn's death."

"If I can."

"If you can."

She and Basil stood on the front porch watching until I turned the corner. I stopped at the main gate of the campus to ask the guard for directions to the Presbyterian cemetery.

ELEVEN

Ms. Kiefner had lulled me into a false security with the morning flight. My return trip was on a commuter airline listed in the phone book next to the bus companies. Our twin-engine turboprop rode the evening sky like a small boat in heavy seas. I turned out to be a lousy sailor. I took a cab from the airport to spite the firm, the Carteret Corporation, and the world. It was a bad decision. My driver was a young man who still had something to prove, and I slid from one side of the cab's broad seat to the other, thinking of the distress bag I'd left on the plane.

I was still in the chair closest to the door of my apartment when the phone rang. The caller was Ms. Kiefner, and I found a second during my initial surprise to wonder if she was calling to apologize or to gloat. Neither, a fresher mind would have told me. Business before pleasure for Ms. Kiefner.

She had called to inform me that Mildred Tucker had agreed to see me the following day and that Mr. Ohlman wanted to talk with me on a very important matter. Yes, Ms. Kiefner. She gave me a phone number for Harry that I didn't recognize and told me to call him at nine. Good night, Ms. Kiefner.

While I waited for nine, I stood my borrowed photographs on the kitchen table. Following examples set in the racier paperbacks I'd studied as a boy, I made myself a drink before sitting down to deduce. I don't know what I was expecting. Psychic emanations, perhaps. Most of what I felt was the warm, drowsy influence of the scotch.

The only thought the photographs produced was the unsatisfying conclusion that my principals had been attractive and well-to-do people. Superficial criticism of detective fiction written between the World Wars generally touched on the artificial quality of upper-class murder, with its arcane motives and passionless movements. According to this view, a real murder is something done by a lunatic to a stranger with no warning or motive or cryptic clues scattered about.

Now I had my own murders, or possible murders, with suspect and victims too privileged and the whole thing too much like S. S. Van Dine for me to feel comfortable. Robert did it in the conservatory with a silver candlestick, Inspector.

At that point in my wanderings, I thought of something Mrs. Parnell had told me, something I'd wanted to hear. Lynn Baxter had switched her affections to William before he had inherited the Carteret pile.

I told myself, as I watched the last of my ice melt, that I would resist the temptation to look for secret passages. I wouldn't let myself be distracted by the money and the plane and the bank. I'd hold instead to the people. If there was any truth behind the story, if Robert loved Lynn or she loved William or he loved himself, I would find it and follow it, and it would keep me safe from mysterious strangers and poison darts.

The kitchen timer I'd set went off, telling me that it was nine. Harry's unfamiliar phone number had an unfamiliar voice to answer it. "Gauthier residence," the voice said.

I asked, politely, for Harry.

"One moment."

The veneer on the voice and the light laughter and conversation I could hear in the background seemed to make my bargain scotch burn a little more than usual. I forced the last swallow down as the other phone was picked up.

"Owen?" Harry asked.

"Sorry to bother you," I said.

"Don't worry about it, Owen. This call is part of a larger plan designed to excuse me from the action." Harry had been drinking, too.

"What are you playing, charades?"

"Bridge. Fortunately our hostess always has an odd person around to watch over your shoulder and sigh when you lead the wrong card. My place has already been taken. Did you learn anything interesting in Albany?"

"Robert and William looked alike."

"They were brothers, Owen."

"You said interesting, not important."

"Let me rephrase."

I jumped in first. "It's going to take me some time to work it all in," I said, "if all of it even fits." I was too tired to do a warm-up for Harry's act.

"Okay. I understand." The understanding had cost Harry some part of his good humor. "I wasn't primarily interested in a report anyway. I was just hoping we'd gotten lucky. I'm afraid I've got some bad news, Owen. Lawrence Bonsett seems to have developed more clout."

It took my off-duty mind a second to connect the name with the famous Carteret Corporation legal department.

"He's given us a deadline for submitting the report," Harry said. "I'm afraid it's tomorrow."

"That's impossible."

"You know that and I know that and I'd be willing to bet that Bonsett knows it too."

I talked for a while because it was my turn. "It doesn't make sense," I said. "Why reopen the investigation at all if they're afraid of finding something?"

"I've been thinking, Owen. Maybe you're right. Maybe Bonsett's orders aren't coming from Carteret. After all, the legal department reports to Carolyn Vernia." Harry didn't really mind my playing Paul Drake, as long as I let him be Perry Mason.

"Why would she even be interested?"

"Carl Vernia." His good humor was returning with his enthusiasm. "He's the only one who really profited from William's death. Carolyn may know that her father could be implicated."

The specter of Agatha Christie was rising again. I was tempted to ask Harry if Carl had used a candlestick, but restraint prevailed. It was bad for our relationship to have so many of our conversations accompanied by alcohol. "You could be right," I said.

"Somebody in the organization may have stumbled across evidence linking Vernia with William Carteret's death and passed it along to Robert Carteret. That would answer a lot of questions."

And create as many unanswered ones, I thought. What could this evidence possibly be? Carl Vernia's 1941 appointment calendar, perhaps. Thursday, 10:45, sabotage plane.

I decided to change the subject. "Did you know that Mildred Tucker had called in?"

"Yes," Harry said.

"I'd still like to talk with her. She may be our last chance."

"There's no time, Owen."

"I may be able to convince them to give us an extension."

"Convince who?"

"Whom." That was a good question. Something in Harry's earlier logic had found a home. "Carolyn Vernia, I guess."

"Do you want to tell me how?"

"I don't think so, Harry."

They must have heard his sigh back at the bridge table.

"I'm beginning to wish I'd stayed with the cards," he said. "You may be right, though. Foreknowledge might not be called for in this situation. For the records, I probably won't be in tomorrow till noon."

"Thanks."

On my way to the bedroom I laid the two photographs facedown on the table. I didn't want any emanations to bother my sleep. "Good night," I said aloud.

TWELVE

MILDRED TUCKER, NÉE FELL, Robert Carteret's almost wife, lived in New Jersey, in the northwestern corner that had escaped the prosperity and the blight of the New York-to-Philadelphia corridor. Her actual address, Riding Creek, told me nothing. Tommy was pleased that I didn't recognize it. He gave me the keys to one of his better cars and told me it was about an hour's drive west on I-80. I wasted the hour sightseeing. Looking back, I can see that my approach to Mildred Tucker was remarkably careless. In a way, I had been careless from the start. Throughout my Carteret wanderings, the only pretense I had been conscious of or concerned about was my own. Now, I was to have that consciousness raised.

Riding Creek was yet another New York bedroom. Three or four good-sized subdivisions were spread around an aging shopping center that doubled as the bus depot. A person commuting between it and New York every day could be forgiven for wondering what had happened to the plan.

The Tucker home was a modest ranch with a worn front lawn that suggested kids. There was a station wagon in the driveway with its hood up. I parked in the street and walked up the drive. As if on cue, a man stepped from in front of the wagon, blocking my way. I was reminded of my meeting with Gus Warden. The man wasn't like Warden physically and he wasn't much older than fifty, but his hands were covered with grease.

"What do you want?" he asked. He was tall and thin and he held his greasy hands away from his body in a way that suggested a gunfighter.

"My name is Owen Keane."

That didn't seem to worry him. "I'm Frank Tucker," he said.

I hadn't counted on meeting Mildred's second husband, which was only my first mistake. I didn't have time to objectively examine the awkwardness of the moment, but I felt it just the same.

"I have an appointment with your wife," I said.

"I know. I want you to talk to me instead. I want you to tell me what this is all about."

Something in his tone seemed affected. I decided that it was important to know if he was worried about his wife or the future of the monthly check. "If you really don't know why I'm here," I said, "I think you'd better ask Mrs. Tucker."

"I don't have to do that. My wife doesn't keep anything from me."

Not anymore, I thought. "I didn't come about the trust fund."

"I don't give a damn about any trust fund, if that's what you call it. You can take that money and go to hell. And tell Robert Carteret that he'd better leave my wife alone."

Tucker was red in the face from shouting his short speech, and I was starting to believe him. He still wasn't tough, but he was angry. The trust money was a sore point, but his feelings seemed to be with his wife. I felt better about him for that.

He took a step toward me. "I think you'd better leave," he said. I hadn't been in a fight since my freshman year in college. That one had been with Harry, and I found the memory of it irritating, as I had lost.

"I'm not going yet," I said. "I didn't come here to relive the school yard. I came to speak with your wife. She worked for Robert Carteret in 1951. That's all I'm interested in. I don't want to upset her or threaten her. I just want to ask her some questions. What you do about the trust fund is your own business."

He chewed on that while I considered my options. It didn't take me long. I was no longer worried about being bounced to my rented car. His hesitation told me that defense was his whole act. But I knew I wouldn't talk my way into the house. I couldn't explain my interest in Robert Carteret to Tucker in twenty-five words or less, and I couldn't undo with talk whatever damage to his pride my intrusion had caused.

We waited like bad actors trying to remember the next line. It turned out to be Mildred Tucker's cue. She opened the front door and called to me. "Mr. Keane? For heaven's sake, come in."

Her commonplace voice had a dampening effect. Tucker's gaze shifted from me to the ground, and I felt as though I could move again. I stepped onto the worn grass and crossed to the front porch. Mrs. Tucker watched me until I reached the top step, then she turned her back on me and entered the house.

The living room was small and dark and had the same signs of heavy traffic as the yard. The decorations were as personal as any mail order catalog. They included a plaster wall hanging of praying hands and a macramé owl. I felt at ease with the room and with the mixed food odors coming from the back of the house. I recognized the setting: a home so heavily used that the traditional functions of the rooms are blurred and meals drag out and overlap.

Mildred Tucker took the room's only chair and I was left with a low couch.

"I hope my husband wasn't rude," she said. She was a small woman. Like her house, she had been given a worn look by constant and overlapping demands. Her face was attractive without having any striking features. I gave her the benefit of the doubt on her blond hair.

"He was upset," I said. "I'm sorry if I've caused you any trouble."

"I'm sure you haven't," she said. I realized then that she didn't see me as a principal in the action. I was just an arm of Robert Carteret, reaching out to screw up her life. I almost wished that that were true.

"I'm not here about the payments," I said.

Her look told me that it was no longer an important point. "You're from the firm that manages the trust," she said.

"Yes."

"What are you anyway, a lawyer?"

"No," I said, "just a person who asks questions." The lack of meaning in my answer was displayed plainly on Mrs. Tucker's face, and I felt my standard embarrassment at having to explain myself. It occurred to me that Lois Parnell hadn't asked for a title or explanation, and I found that memory even more embarrassing. "I'm doing some research concerning the Carteret family," I began.

Mildred cut me off. "I'm not a member," she said. "I wasn't good enough for them."

"I'd like to ask you some questions," I said.

"Thanks for the explanation."

I was becoming one of "them" by repeating their lack of respect. I found that I was looking at her shoes. They were boxy leathers made to look like sneakers. "I'm sorry," I said. "My work requires discretion."

"You don't have much talent for it." She had turned her head and was looking toward the front windows.

"You should have told him a long time ago," I said. She turned back and her dull, flat eyes flashed at me as though I had just appeared out of the air before her. She opened her mouth to speak, but her head sank slowly instead and she began to cry, quietly. Her chin rested on her chest and her head bobbed up and down.

"Please," I said, "I'm sorry."

Her effort to choke off her sobbing made her whole body shake. When she spoke, her words were divided by sharp intakes of breath. "Who are you?"

"Someone who means you no harm in spite of all the damage I've done." I thought of Lois Parnell again. She could have told me the name of the B-movie I was suddenly quoting. "I'm investigating the death of Robert's brother, William. He died in a plane crash in 1941."

Instead of asking me to explain the connection to herself, Mrs. Tucker revealed some interest. "He's well again, then," she said.

An unfortunate "who" came to my lips, but I caught it in time. "My instructions are from Robert Carteret himself," I said. To give me time to think, I produced Carteret's letter for her to read.

"You've heard of William Carteret," I said, tentatively.

"Yes." She answered without looking up from the letter.

"Did Robert tell you about him?"

"No. Pete did."

"Pete?"

"Peter Gregson. He was the gardener at the estate. The grounds keeper, I guess you'd call him."

"He saw William Carteret take off on the morning he was killed."

"Yes. He told me about it more than once. He was proud of it for some reason. But that was the whole story. He just looked up from his work and saw the plane. No one knew what happened after that."

"Did you ever discuss it with Robert?"

"Oh, no. Robert never mentioned it to me or anyone else. Dr. Schiel believed that it was part of Robert's illness."

Mrs. Tucker was moving fast now, assuming more background knowledge than I really had. I decided to play along with her and hope for the best.

"How did Dr. Schiel think it fit together?" I asked.

She didn't miss a beat. "I'm not sure. He'd worked with neurological disorders during the war. He didn't believe that Robert's wounds were sufficient to produce his degree of trauma and the duration of his withdrawal." The tone of her voice made the words sound like a quote. "And it fit the peculiar part of Robert's loss of memory. It extended back before Anzio, to well before the war. Dr. Schiel said he may have locked out all his pain at once."

She paused for a moment and looked concerned. I was afraid she was finally going to question my credentials. I was wrong. "Do you know about Lynn Baxter?" she asked.

"She was William's fiancée. She died with him in the plane crash."

"He was in love with her. Robert, I mean. He would have bad nights. He'd toss around in a sweat and wake up screaming and yelling. Her name was one of the things he'd yell."

"Do you remember any of the others?"

She looked more concerned, but she continued. "Some nights he'd cover his head with his arms. Then he'd yell 'No, Robert, no!' over and over again. I don't know why he disassociated like that. It was the only time he'd speak of himself in the third person. With some patients it's pretty common."

"Carteret was sound physically?"

"Yes," Mrs. Tucker said, "very sound." The memory didn't seem to cheer her. "And very attractive. I was too young for a post like that. I really wasn't a nurse yet. I didn't know enough about the emotional side. I thought I could heal him myself. I don't remember how I planned to do it."

She'd made progress with the emotional side of her job since Carteret. She was able to speak of their brief marriage with a clinical detachment. I understood that she was no longer speaking to a researcher. I listened anyway.

"I really don't know how it happened. How I let it happen. I've thought since that Robert took advantage of me, but that might just be the hurt coming out. He was having a good period. He was remembering more and retaining more. I worked with him quite a bit, and he got to know me pretty well. He told me that he'd known me before the war, but that was just a way he had. He didn't like to admit he couldn't remember you. I suppose I had a crush on him, a maternal one anyway. He wanted to escape the house, I know, but he wanted me, too. I know he did. He had a plan to elope, but I didn't want to leave the city. We waited out the license period in a friend's apartment. Those few days are like a dream now when I try to look back. Once we were actually married, it changed. He changed. His good period was over. He became disoriented and listless." She paused for a moment. "He forgot who I was. I was scared. I called Dr. Schiel. Robert and I were together for another hour. I never saw him again.

"I thought I was through as a nurse." She was looking at my shoes now. "I thought I deserved to be. But they never suspended my license."

"They didn't want a scandal," I said.

"I knew that." The statement was an admission of guilt. "And I knew the money was to buy my silence."

She stopped talking and I stopped asking questions. I listened instead to the house. Somewhere behind me there was a loud clock. I identified a muffled crashing sound as the kitchen ice maker. Outside, Frank Tucker was telling someone to stay away from the house. I guessed it was one of the children whose mark was everywhere. His tone was harsh, and it reminded me of the role I was playing in their lives.

"I should be going," I said, standing.

She was surprised. "You've hardly asked me a thing," she said. I understood her to mean that I hadn't learned anything worth the pain I'd caused.

Perhaps another gram of impersonal research would tip the scale. "What was Dr. Schiel's first name?" I asked.

"Donald."

"Thank you."

Her eyes were wet again. "We mean to stop the money, Mr. Keane."

A real detective would have topped her easily. Just don't stop your lives, Mrs. Tucker. "I'm sorry for everything," I said, instead. Me and everybody else.

Frank Tucker was leaning against the front of his car, considering his concrete. I had the idea that I should let him knock me down, but he no longer looked interested.

"Did you get what you wanted?" he asked.

"More than I wanted."

"Look, I didn't know about Carteret. She told me it was an inheritance. From an uncle." His eyes were red like his wife's and there was grease on his nose. He misread my expression. "Yeah," he said. "But she's a good woman. I think she believed in the uncle herself.

"It's in the house, you know. And the car." He patted the car's grille.

"What was wrong with the engine?" I asked.

"Nothing. Air filter. I was just changing it."

"You're no mechanic."

He looked down at his greasy hands. "Oh, that," he said. "Inspiration of the moment. If I couldn't beat you up, I was going to ruin your suit."

We both smiled. "You're not what I expected," he said.

I gave in to the detective talk. "I'm not even what I expected." I needed the exit line to get me down to my car. I used the driveway to turn around. Tucker was still leaning on his car, but now he was studying the house.

Robert Carteret and I had a lot to answer for in Riding Creek.

THIRTEEN

I RETURNED THE CAR to Tommy and walked to the public library. Because of my mental state, I didn't stop at the Johnson Tyre Building. I'd come back to the city seriously considering Bonsett's deadline as an easy way out. To have spoken my doubts aloud would have caused pieces of Harry to fall down around my ears.

The city looked dirty to me during my walk, but dirty doesn't describe it adequately. The dirt and the rust and the graffiti all seemed part of an enormous design whose pattern was indiscernible. Any message I left would disappear against that background. My own track was overlaid as I walked. No one in the heavy sidewalk traffic would remember me in ten minutes. The city made me feel that the traces of 1941 I'd found were illusions and the testimony I'd received impossible fiction.

One piece of that fiction, Mrs. Tucker's story, had taken the smooth, sandy bottom from under my day. To keep myself from sinking in the ooze, I played Harry's part. I told myself not to imagine plots, not to see mystery where there was only misunderstanding, not to see divine intent in the fall of every leaf. I told myself that people were basically nice and that the elements of the universe tended toward unity. It might have been that I was crossing Forty-second Street, but none of my pep talk seemed remotely probable.

I arrived at the library just after two. I stopped at a bank of four wooden phone booths, which stood on the third-floor landing like an historical exhibit, and wrestled Dr. Schiel's number from the rack of hinged directories.

The woman who answered his phone had an irritated voice. She wouldn't ask the doctor to come to the phone, so I tried to make an appointment. She treated the request as a joke, and told me that Dr. Schiel only saw patients referred by other physicians. It was then that I stepped boldly to the front of the researcher ranks.

"It's really a kind of referral," I said. "Sort of a family matter, too. My father told me to call Dr. Schiel. He and Dad go back a long way. It's pretty urgent."

"What is your father's name?"

"Robert Carteret," I said.

"One moment." It was the kind of moment that passes very slowly for amateur liars. The receptionist returned with an even more irritated voice. "The doctor will see you at four," she said. "That's after normal office hours, so please be prompt."

"I really appreciate..."

"What is your first name?"

"William."

It had been one of my better phone calls, but I felt myself sinking again as I hung up. Mildred Tucker had made odd pieces of all my information and given me Dr. Schiel as the oddest piece of all. His role was unclear. Guardian, warden, physician. I had no idea which.

I said before that Harry and Marilyn were right when they accused me of fantasizing. They were wrong in thinking that I believed my fantasies, my hypothetical realities. Prior to Dr. Schiel, I'd often thought I would have been happier if I could believe them. But I believed in the doctor. I believed that Robert Carteret's life-style was not eccentricity but sentence. I believed that Dr. Schiel understood the distinction. None of it made me any happier.

I decided to call Harry after all. I wanted the name-brand common sense treatment. If that failed, I wanted him to stay by the phone while I kept my appointment. What I got was Ms. Kiefner, who told me that Harry was in conference. I thanked her and hung up and regretted it immediately. It seemed important at that moment to establish some real communication with the woman, to get her to recognize my existence. The fact that I hadn't accomplished that compromised me. I knew I wasn't even a notation on her yellow telephone pad. I felt as though I were invisible.

A rapping on the phone booth door reminded me that I was not. The specific message was delivered by a stout lady in a gumdrop-shaped hat. She presented me with two alternatives, the second of which was to "get off the pot."

I went to the catalog room to see Marilyn, but she was off somewhere following a trail of her own. I left her a peace offering in the form of a research question: "Who was Phaeton?" Then I wandered into the North Hall. I was looking for an impersonal introduction to Dr. Schiel. In the American Medical Association's *Directory of Medical Specialists*, I found him.

SCHIEL, DONALD H. Cert P&N 52. Born 16 Camden, N.J. MD Johns Hop 38, Intern St Vincents Hosp NYC 39-41, Res Neur 41-42, Res Neur Menninger Vet Hosp NYC 45-49, Asst Dir Dept Neuropsy 50-55, Asst Clen Prof Psy Cornell Med Center 52-59, Res Neur NYU Med Center 59. Capt AUS 42-45. pub *Battlefield Neurology* 50. AMA-APA.

Dr. Schiel's career had been all start and no finish. I photocopied the entry and checked the card catalog for Schiel's book. It directed me to the fourth floor, unfamiliar territory.

Battlefield Neurology didn't have a dustcover photograph of its author or a biographical blurb. It didn't even have one of the new antiseptic computer checkout cards in the back pocket. Its yellowed, hand-stamped card told me that the book hadn't left the building since 1962. Score one for John Hyatt and the English majors.

I took the book to an outside aisle where there were little Formica cubicles for reading. A couple of teenagers were exploring alternate uses in a cubicle nearby. They gave me a look that suggested I wasn't welcome, but I sat down anyway. I wanted the company.

The book had been published in 1950, when Schiel was thirty-four. Its introduction told me that Schiel intended to draw a line between the two general causes of "war-related mental dysfunction: physical and emotional trauma." Schiel, a neurologist, seemed to come down on the side of physical damage to the brain and nervous system. He didn't dismiss what he termed "hysterical reactions," but he wouldn't allow their consideration to "interfere with the treatment of identified physical impairments." He knew his subject, he seemed to say. He'd been there.

Schiel mentioned a Warner-Komlanc syndrome as an example he would consider in detail. It was characterized, he said, by retrograde amnesia and continuing "cognitive difficulties." I liked the sound of that, so I flipped to the index to find more material.

Warner-Komlanc was a product of a mixed marriage. Warner was a nineteenth-century neurologist who had studied memory loss in victims of head injuries and stroke. Komlanc was a more contemporary psychologist who saw the syndrome as a problem of motivation. To him, the disease was best understood as a loss of the will to think, associate, or plan ahead, caused by the emotional shock of an accident or illness. It seemed to be a disease made to test Schiel's thesis of division.

Schiel introduced the case of a young soldier who had been wounded in Italy. He called him C.C. I flipped hurriedly through my notebook to confirm that Robert Carteret's middle name was Charles. C.C. had suffered a shrapnel wound to the region of the brain called the hippocampus. He had survived the wound and battlefield surgery, but his memory was "permanently impaired." At first his amnesia had been complete; he could remember nothing of his past and retain nothing new. His doctors had prompted him with the little information they'd had—his name, his hometown—until he had finally begun to contribute prewar memories. A period of total amnesia extended back two years before he'd been wounded.

Prior to the blank period and after it his memory was undependable. C.C. could remember isolated incidents in great detail and learn new names and skills. He suffered from occasional bad periods, however, during which he would lose any new material he'd acquired. These "dysfunctional periods" seemed to puzzle Schiel. He noted them as areas of possible future research, theorizing vaguely that the alternate brain structures C.C. had adopted to channel and store information had failed him.

Schiel wrote well, or perhaps his subject matter alone absorbed me. I hadn't noticed that an hour had passed and my teenage company had left. I went to look for Marilyn, and to hide from four o'clock.

FOURTEEN

I PASSED THE PHONE BOOTH exhibit on the stairs, and it reminded me of a question I'd considered during my reading. I called Mildred Tucker's number, half expecting her husband and another misunderstanding. Instead, a very young female voice answered.

"Hello," she said.

"Hello. May I please speak to your mother?"

"My mother isn't here. She's at school. Know what?"

"What?"

"I started school this year."

"Kindergarten?"

"No. I'm not old enough. I'm four."

"Oh."

"Know what?"

"What?"

"I can spell my name and I can spell Jesus' name."

"You're all set."

"Yep. You know what?"

There was the sound of an extension being picked up. Mildred Tucker came on the line. She used a tone of voice I hadn't heard during my visit. "Sarah, are you playing on the phone?"

"No. I'm talking."

"She was telling me about her school, Mrs. Tucker. This is Owen Keane."

"Sarah, honey, you hang up now, okay?"

"Okay. Good-bye."

"Good-bye," I said.

Mildred and I both waited for the sound of Sarah's receiver and then for something else. I weakened first. "Your daughter told me you were at school."

"Sarah is my granddaughter, Mr. Keane."

"Oh." Marilyn had been right. The Carteret trail was colder than I'd made myself believe. "I have another question if you have a minute, Mrs. Tucker. I'm sorry to bother you again."

"What is it?"

"You mentioned that Robert Carteret had wanted you two to elope. Do you remember where he wanted to go?"

There was a scratchy silence on the line, and I waited for a dial tone. Instead, Mrs. Tucker said: "Maryland. Years ago you could be married pretty easily in Maryland. On a short license. I think it only took a day. Kind of like what they have out west now. In Vegas, I guess."

"I didn't know that."

"Before your time. I have to go now."

"Thank you," I said. "Good-bye."

Marilyn had returned to the catalog room and left again since my last visit. A sympathetic coworker with half-moon reading glasses told me that Marilyn was relieving the clerk in economics and public affairs on the second floor. I backtracked, checking my watch and my resolve every few steps.

The economics material was tucked into the end of the building's south wing. Its reception area was actually out in the hall, in a small corner claimed by a half wall of old wood and leaded glass. The wall's Gothic woodwork and something in its fragile nature reminded me of a confessional. I walked past it and between walls lined with filing cabinets. Marilyn sat at a small desk at the head of the hallway, which was backed by a naked steam radiator and an open window. The light from the window made her expression impossible to read until I was standing at the desk.

"Hello, Keane," she said. "*Directory of Medical Specialists* sounds like a new assignment."

"How did you know about that?" I asked.

"You touched one of the strands of my web." She was in a good mood, and it suited her. Her color was high, and I suspected that she'd been beach walking again. Even her combative hair looked good to me, which told me that I was happy to see her. I hated to spoil the moment.

"Same assignment, Marilyn. Different angle."

The temperature in the hallway seemed to drop a degree or two as Marilyn's smile faded. Her new expression confirmed my deduction about her reaction to the Carteret story. She looked as though she felt sorry for me. I would have preferred a repeat of her earlier anger.

"Did you get my note?" I asked.

"Yes," Marilyn said. She pulled an index card from her shirt pocket. "Phaeton was a character from Greek mythology. He was the son of Helios, the sun god, who was thought to ride across the sky in a flaming chariot. One day Phaeton borrowed the chariot, but he couldn't handle the sun god's horses. He scorched the earth before he fell to his death." She looked up from the card. "He screwed up, Keane. He took on too much. He came down hard." She paused to stare that observation home.

"And I found a quote from Shakespeare. *Richard II.* 'Down, down I come, like glist'ring Phaeton, wanting the manage of unruly jades.'"

She handed me the card. "Anything else?"

"Yes," I said, "a favor."

"If it's a date, I'm kind of booked up."

"How about cancellations?"

"Is it a date, Keane?"

"No. I'm going to see a man in a little while, a doctor. I'll write his name down."

"On one of my slips?"

"I'll give you Harry's number, too. Harry Ohlman. He's the man I work for."

"I know that. What is this all about?"

"If you don't hear from me by six, I'd like you to call Harry and tell him where I've gone."

"I'll tell him you've gone to Oz, how's that?"

"I'm serious."

"So am I. See? I'm not smiling anymore. I was smiling when you came in, but I'm not anymore." Neither was I. "Look, Keane, I'm not going to indulge you. If you ever want to do serious research again, fine, I'll help you. If you decide to live in the real world, great, give me a call. But if you want to live in a world of your own, get used to being alone. Play Don Quixote all you want. Just don't ask me to be Dulcinea. I don't owe you any favors. We're all paid up."

"Then I'll owe you," I said.

"No." Marilyn banged the desktop hard enough to make its phone jump. "I don't want my name and address pinned to your lapel. Is that clear enough? If I wanted children, I'd adopt."

"Can I at least tell you about it? The story isn't as simple now as the one I told you before."

"I know all about William Carteret," Marilyn said. "I know about his fiancée. I know about his damn brother. I know what the Carteret Corporation earned last year."

"How do you know?" I asked, taken aback.

"I checked the lint in your pants cuffs. The point is, I didn't find God's fingerprints on any of it. And I didn't find any deep, dark mysteries. I found names and dates. That's all. You're off on a tangent, Keane. And if you don't come back now, you might never be able to."

"You looked it up," I said, amazed.

"I didn't find this dream world you're weaving for yourself, do you understand? I don't believe any of that."

I pulled Robert Carteret's letter of instruction from my pocket, hoping to stall with it as I had with Mildred Tucker. Marilyn wouldn't look at it. She kept watching my eyes, trying to decide which way I'd move next.

"This is Carteret's letter asking us to look into his brother's death," I said. "I'm not sure about it anymore. I don't think that's what he wanted us, me, to do. I think it's a code, a message in a bottle. This man I'm going to see, Dr. Schiel, may be able to tell me what it means. Or he may be the man Carteret is trying to get around. I don't know." Marilyn opened her mouth to speak. "And you don't believe any of it," I said. "I understand. I'm not asking you to believe. I'm asking for a favor."

The slip I'd used as notepaper was a two-part form, white on yellow. I pulled it apart and held the white section out to her. She took the slip, crumpled it, and dropped it, all in a quick, fluid motion. I admired it. I put the yellow part in my vest pocket because I was suddenly sentimental.

On my way out of the library, I decided that I would reexamine my theory of human relationships when time permitted. For the moment, I put one foot in front of the other and headed east.

FIFTEEN

I ARRIVED at Dr. Schiel's office just before four. It was
on the sixth floor of an unnamed office building
across the street from the New York University Medical Center. The elevator rode quietly and with little
indication of motion. I was alone in the elevator and
alone in the sixth-floor hallway where the elevator left
me. On the deep pile carpet I was as silent as the elevator had been. That thought made me look quickly
over my shoulder as I walked down the hall. I thought
Dr. Schiel's door was locked at first, but it was only
unusually heavy. The large brass handle was cool to
my touch. I marked it with the moist print of my palm.

The receptionist's face didn't light up at my entrance, which was a shame. It was a very nice face. She
wore a white dress, but it wasn't a nurse's uniform. At
least it wasn't buttoned like one. I managed to smile
at how detectivelike my observations were becoming.
She smiled back, from reflex.

"Mr. Carteret?" she asked.

"Yes."

"The doctor should be able to see you right away."
She was working on that assumption anyway. Her
handbag was on the top of the desk in front of her and
her topcoat lay conspicuously beside it. She lifted the
receiver of her phone, pressed a button, and hung up
without waiting for a reply. I smiled again for no particular reason.

Dr. Schiel appeared in the doorway to the receptionist's left without so much as the sound of a foot-
step to announce him. He was taller than I, and
heavier. Not a fat man, but large. He had white hair
that was thin on top and combed straight back, and
white, muttonchop sideburns. His face was lined
without looking weathered, and it had a pink color,
accentuated, I decided, by his hair. He wore a long
white coat, opened to display a shirt and tie of identical green, and blue trousers. His broad smile made
the whole collection seem like a logical unit.

"Hello, Mr. Carteret," Dr. Schiel said. He had a
deep voice that gained speed as he spoke. I had the
impression that he would break into laughter easily.

"Hello," I said.

"What seems to be the problem?"

The waiting-room interrogation made me feel like
I'd lost before I'd begun. "My head hurts," I said.

We looked at each other over the quality carpeting
until the receptionist coughed. "If you don't mind,
Dr. Schiel," she said.

Dr. Schiel looked as if he didn't mind anything.
"Sorry, Barbara," he said. "Didn't mean to keep you.
You can get Mr. Carteret's history on his second visit.
Good night."

Her smile flashed on and off as she breezed past me.
I stood in my original position, waiting for the sound
of the heavy door closing behind her. It didn't make
any sound, naturally.

"Come in, Mr. Carteret, come in. I don't mind
telling you that your visit is the high point of my day."
He led me past an impressive examining room and into
an office that was surprisingly small. He squeezed be-

hind the desk, and I sat down in front of it, pretending to study the diplomas and awards on the walls.

"Is there too much in it or not enough?" Schiel asked me.

"Pardon me?"

"Your head. You said it hurt. I wanted to know if there was too much in it or not enough. It was a joke."

"Oh," I said. I was trying to decide if I'd lost control of the situation or just never had it to begin with. His cherub smile seemed to be in control now.

"You don't look so good," he said.

"I haven't eaten today." It was the first time I'd even thought of it.

"I hope that isn't a reflection on your ability to pay my fee. That's another joke. You Carterets have never had a problem paying your way. At least your father never had. How is he, by the way?"

"That's what I came to find out." That announcement didn't affect Schiel's good humor.

"I guess I should ask about your mother, too," he said. "How is she? Or maybe I should ask, who is she?"

"Her name is Mildred Fell," I said. That reply didn't take away the doctor's rosy smile either, but it froze it in place for a moment.

"I'll put you down as having good reflexes," he said. "I'd almost forgotten about Mildred." He shifted his weight and crossed his legs, an operation that made his swivel chair cry out. "Mildred Fell." He studied the wall above my head and scratched one sideburn reflectively. "Sweet girl, Mildred," he finally said, "but not very bright. Forgive me for speaking frankly, but you've probably noticed it yourself."

"No," I said. "I take after her side of the family."
Irritation was coming to my aid, an irritation caused
by his warm appreciation of my position. "I'd like to
ask you some questions, Doctor."

"About your father?"

"About Robert Carteret."

"Unless you can prove you're his son, which I'd
love to see, I'm afraid I'll have to decline. Confiden-
tiality, you know."

I decided I'd have to put up with his smile. "How
about another patient?" I asked. "Textbook case.
You called him C.C."

Schiel sat up straight. "You read my book?"

"Parts of it."

"What did you think of it? Forgive me for asking,
but I was really proud of that book. I had more than
a little of the would-be author in me back then."

"You write well," I said. I had no idea what he
wanted to hear. "You should have kept at it."

He laughed at that. "I don't know," he said. "I like
to think that I was one of that large group of men
whose best work came out in a gush just after the war.
Sort of the Norman Mailer of neurology. Most soldiers experience an emotional letdown after the
shooting stops. My high was extended for a year or
two. At least that's what I tell myself. Makes me feel
better about being lazy."

A banging noise in the hall startled me.

"Relax," Schiel said. A moment later a man appeared in the doorway. He wore matching gray shirt
and pants and carried a bucket.

"Excuse me," the man said, turning to leave.

"Be done in half an hour or so, Bill," Schiel said.
"Cleaning people bother you, son?"

"No," I said. As a matter of fact, Bill made me feel better, less like a candidate for an impromptu lobotomy.

"I am lazy, though," Schiel said, picking up his previous thought, "or jealous of my free time. But that's not really why I never wrote again. Once burned, you know. That first book was more trouble than it was worth. I wouldn't be boring you with this, but it brings us back to C.C. You did want to talk about C.C., didn't you?"

"Yes."

"Are you really interested in any of this? I notice you're not taking notes."

"I have a good memory."

He slapped an open palm on his desktop in pleasure.

"You may be a born straight man," he said. "Listen to this transition. A memory is the only thing C.C. didn't have. Like that? Let's test your memory, Mr. Carteret. After all, this was supposed to be an examination. Tell me about C.C."

"He was wounded in Italy. Shell fragment. Hippocampus. He ended up with retrograde amnesia and no retention. Warner-Komlanc syndrome."

"I still shudder when I hear that name. Anything else?"

"You had a theoretical bone to pick. More accurate distinction between hysterical and physical dysfunction for proper diagnosis and effective treatment."

"Well stated. Yes. I was pretty militant about that."

"Is that how you were burned?"

"Yes, and by our friend C.C. as a matter of fact. To be more accurate, C.C. was only the petard with which

I hoisted myself. That still isn't very clear, is it? What I'm trying to say is, my diagnosis of C.C. was incorrect. That was my unpardonable sin."

"How was your diagnosis incorrect?"

"I was determined, in my arrogance, to treat C.C. as a victim of physical trauma exclusively. Not to muddle his recovery by asking him whether or not he hated his father. You'd be surprised how much of that we had back then. My resentment of psychoanalysis was itself an emotional reaction. I couldn't admit that the notebook could be better than the knife. Of course, they were still in the dark ages in those days. I put that forward in my own defense. They've come a long way since I worked with survivors of Korea and Vietnam, and my outlook has changed, let me tell you. I've given up knowing all the answers. I take help now from anyone who offers it."

Schiel's gaze had drifted back to the ceiling. Now, he looked down at me. "Has anyone ever told you that you inspire rambling? I think it's that poker expression you have. Your face poses the same temptation as a blank sheet of paper."

"C.C. had serious emotional problems?" I asked.

"It's depressing to have an eloquent speech sifted away for a pebble of fact. Yes, C.C.'s nice stable background turned out to have flaws. An unhappy love affair was the most glaring. Unfortunately, his personal history came to us from business associates of his father. He had no close family left. These men were a little coy, as it later turned out.

"C.C. was progressing nicely, and my book was receiving some very gratifying attention when havoc struck. He ran off with his nurse, married the poor girl, and spent a romantic weekend at the Essex Hotel. When we finally found them, C.C. was back at square one, and so was I. I never wrote a second book."

"Or a retraction of your first."

"No." Schiel's smile became one-sided and he examined me more closely than he had since we'd left the reception area. His eyes were pale blue, and their whites were clear. They looked into me as he spoke. "No, I never made a formal retraction. C.C.'s guardians, one in particular, took the first book badly. It was important to them that C.C. be cured. If his condition proved permanent, it was important that he appeared cured. I was never permitted to publish on the case again." He looked away from me and back toward his indirect lighting. "As a matter of fact, I was taken off the case altogether shortly after the elopement."

"You're not his doctor now?"

"No. Surely you knew that, Mister... What is your real name, incidentally?"

"Owen Keane."

"Any relation to that old radio detective Mr. Keene, 'tracer of lost persons'?"

"No."

"Too bad. No I haven't been C.C.'s doctor since 1952. Until a year or so ago, I hadn't even been to visit him. He had a change of guardians a few years back. The new adminstration is more enlightened, and they were worried about C.C.'s condition. It has deteriorated, I'm afraid. So I was brought back as a consultant of sorts. They certainly didn't brief you very well."

"They didn't brief me at all."

"For whom do you work?"

"Ohlman, Ohlman, and Pulsifer, Attorneys at Law."

"Can you prove that?"

"Would you like to see my group insurance card?"

Schiel looked genuinely puzzled. "Whom do you represent?" he asked.

The answer to that seemed silly, considering what Schiel had just told me, but silly was a feeling I'd learned to live with. "Robert Carteret," I said.

"Meaning the Carteret Corporation."

"We were engaged through the corporation. I represent Mr. Carteret."

"Easier said than done, Owen. You don't mind if I call you that, I hope. I'm pretty quick on my feet normally, but I really need time to think. Engaged through the corporation? How did that happen? The consequences of our actions are really amazing sometimes."

"I don't understand," I said.

"You don't?" His patient expression reminded me that he had also been a teacher. I reran his last speech, and it brought me to the worn piece of paper I carried in my pocket. I produced Carteret's letter. Schiel's light blue eyes showed interest, but not surprise.

"You might like to read this," I said. "It's my letter of instruction."

Schiel took the letter, still folded, laid it across his forehead, and closed his eyes. "Dear Sir," Schiel said, "This is to empower you to investigate the plane crash which claimed the life of my brother, William Carteret, and his fiancée on October something, 1941. I require all the details that can be determined with dispatch and discretion." Schiel opened his eyes and smiled broadly. "How's that?" he asked. "The amazing Schiel, assisted by Owen Keane."

"Why?" I asked.

"Whimsy. You may not have noticed it, but I'm a whimsical man. Seeing Carteret again was a shock. He's aged rather well, in a way. He actually looks like the chief executive officer he's supposed to be. But Carteret the personality, what's left of him, is in great pain.

"It felt like a reunion at first, any reunion. Shake with the mistakes of your youth, and all that. I had the silly idea that he might remember me, but that was just vanity. I felt sorry for him, in a way I hadn't after the war. We're both old men now, so I guess I was feeling sorry for myself, too. I don't know what I'd really like to know after sixty-five years, what single revelation would make me a peaceful man. I thought I knew what Carteret's revelation was. Hence the letter."

"You believe that his brother's death is the cause of his emotional problems?"

"And the death of his brother's fiancée. You couldn't investigate one without investigating the other. So in a sense, Owen, you're working for me. I just don't understand why you're being allowed to. Any thoughts on that?"

I took the letter from the top of Schiel's desk and placed it back in my pocket. "Maybe Carteret's new guardians are as curious as you. What can you tell me about Carl Vernia?"

"Nothing good. He's the villain of the piece from my point of view. Let me see. He was a small man, and not just by my physical standards. Stiff and sour and very close. A regular Calvin Coolidge. Vernia withheld the business of William Carteret from me until it was too late. Pretty bald omission, too, considering that he saw Carteret on the morning of his last flight.''

"Who told you that?''

"Vernia, and without apology. He was almost frank after the Essex Hotel incident. For a time. If he'd confided in me earlier, well, who can say?''

Schiel had picked up a pen, and as he spoke he doodled on his blotter. His drawings were circles containing smaller and smaller circles. His eyes had taken on a wary look that I didn't like. I took a guess at the cause of his sudden shift in mood.

"You suspected Carteret's emotional trouble before the elopement," I said. "Mildred Fell remembered your suspicions, something about the wound being insufficient to produce Carteret's degree of withdrawal.''

Schiel's one-sided smile returned. "I don't remember ever addressing her on the subject. I must have been thinking aloud.''

"You said before that your misdiagnosis was an unpardonable sin. Who wouldn't pardon you?''

"I wouldn't," he said.

"Because you questioned your thesis and published anyway?''

"And because I hadn't the professional guts to expose Vernia and retract my study. My self-punishment had the effect of a retraction, in a way. By not pursuing my work or even acknowledging inquiries on it, I informed our small community that my research was unreliable. I guess I wrote that letter for myself, too. I owe Robert Carteret.''

"Why did Vernia want Carteret's condition kept secret?''

"I don't think I can add anything to your own speculation on that."

"Did Vernia suspect that Robert was responsible for William's death?"

"No. He seemed confident that Robert had had nothing to do with it. Vernia wasn't a good liar, he couldn't trust his face. I think that was why he was so closemouthed. I'm not saying that he had any firm knowledge on the subject, but I think he really dismissed the old gossip as nonsense."

"Vernia died of a heart attack."

"Yes."

"Did he have a history of heart trouble?"

"None that I heard of. I was never his physician, of course. All I know of his death is what I read in the paper."

Schiel was tapping his pen on the desk now, and I decoded his message as "wrap it up." I tried to think of loose ends. "Do you have copies of Robert's service records?" I asked.

"Nope. Sorry."

"How complete was his memory of the years before his brother's death?"

"Not very complete. Oddly segmented, like that of an old man. He could remember isolated incidents in great detail. He could describe one birthday party, it must have been his ninth or tenth, as though it had happened yesterday. In other areas he couldn't even respond to prompting. You understand that I'm speaking of his condition just after the war. He's much worse now, I'm afraid."

"Did he remember the household staff?"

"No, they were all new. Vernia had closed the house during the war and dismissed the staff. The only one left was a gardener."

"Gregson."

Schiel smiled his rosy smile again. "I'm glad I'm not employing a lazy detective. Gregson first mentioned William Carteret's death to me." He looked at his watch and sat up straight at his desk. "Where do we go from here?" he asked.

I liked the "we," but I could see no practical use for it. "I go to see Carteret's new guardian," I said.

"Carolyn Vernia."

"Yes."

"Good luck. I hope to hear from you again."

We shook hands. "I hope you do, too," I said.

"I've enjoyed our talk, believe it or not." He laughed. "But as I told you, I'm a whimsical man."

Schiel escorted me out of the office. I stopped in the reception area for a last question. "Did you ever see a picture of William Carteret?"

"No," Schiel said. "Odd that you should mention it, but I can't remember ever seeing one around the house."

SIXTEEN

THE CITY WAS GIVING UP the struggle. It was five o'clock, and late enough in the year for the sky to reinforce the idea that five was a natural breaking point in the day. I mingled with the evacuees and tried to come up with a plan. Background noise for my walk was provided by the aggressive traffic and an occasional portable stereo carried by someone who had no other way to declare a space in the city. The sidewalks were dominated by purposeful people, tired, but following a determined path with enough concentration to shut out those around them. Carried along with them were people like myself, who looked for something in faces and storefronts and sunsets because we had not found that distant goal. We searched without heart, avoiding the eyes of other searchers.

I was looking for a particular research assistant. I seriously considered going back to see her. I wanted to tell her that she was wrong, that my plot was real, which shows how little feel I had for our relationship. Telling her I'd imagined the whole thing was a better way out, as long as I could convince her that I'd never do it again. But telling her anything at that moment was impossible. She was probably halfway to Brooklyn. I hadn't the nerve to carry the fight there.

My deadline was passing as I walked. Whatever tenuous claim I had to Robert Carteret's sponsorship was passing with it. My letter of instruction, which I'd been carrying as a talisman, had already turned to dross. I had the feeling that, in exchange, Mildred Tucker and Dr. Schiel had given me something more powerful. And more dangerous.

I worked out my plan in a moment spent standing in front of a drugstore that sold everything but drugs. Its lunch counter was serving coffee and pie to homeless people who had temporarily conceded the sidewalks to the commuters. In a back aisle, I found a box of typing paper with four or five price tags pasted on top of one another, a large manila envelope, and a yellow plastic report cover designed to hold paper with a small clamp.

A girl from the lunch counter came over to the register to take my money. She stayed to watch as I fastened the blank typing paper into the cover.

"In a hurry?" she asked.

"Yes," I said.

"Need a pen?"

"No, thanks." On the envelope, in the upper-left-hand corner, I printed the name and address of my firm. On the front, in large block letters, I added: "Carolyn Vernia" and "Confidential."

The girl was still watching. I smiled. "I could use a cab."

"Good luck, honey," she said.

I lost the time it took me to walk two blocks before I lucked onto a cab that was dropping off a fare. At a red light I opened my blank report to the first page. On it I wrote: "Which Carteret brother are you holding on Long Island?" Beneath that, I inserted my business card.

"What's so funny, mister?" the cab driver asked me. He spoke with a foreign accent I couldn't begin to place. His reflection in the rearview mirror leered at me like an animated version of his registration photograph.

"Nothing really," I said. "I'm just whimsical this evening. It's contagious."

"Uh-huh." His expression told me he was naturally immune.

The Egyptian gates of the Carteret Building were still open, but to enter I had to fight against a strong current of outward-bound bank employees, none of whom knew as much about their boss as I did. The girl at the circular stone desk had been replaced by a uniformed guard. I handed him the sealed envelope, wishing I'd written "rush" or "urgent" on it somewhere. "It's pretty important," I said instead.

The guard had the relaxed look of a retired something else, a soldier or a policeman. I expected an argument, but he smiled at me and waved the envelope at another guard who stood by the elevators. "Run this up to eleven, George," he said.

I stayed to watch until the elevator doors closed. Good luck, George. The sidewalks were still crowded, but I didn't mind. They would thin soon enough. I felt elated, almost high, and not just because I hadn't eaten. I had entered on a desperate venture, and there was a great feeling of relief in that. I had eliminated the pressure of choice. I had also separated myself forcefully from the Carteret Corporation and the associations I had meekly accepted that morning in Riding Creek. Last but not least, I had submitted, I was sure, the most effective report of my career.

I was trying to decide where I would have my celebration dinner, when I remembered Carteret. I probably owed him a report, too, I decided. I would certainly need his willing help shortly. I crossed the street to a hotel and rented a lobby phone.

Harry jumped on the first ring. "Ohlman, Ohlman, and Pulsifer," he said.

"What are you doing answering the phone?" I asked.

"Owen, where are you?"

"Phone booth. Berkshire lobby, Fifty-second and Madison."

"God damn it. You had us worried."

"Who's 'us'?"

"Me, I mean. I'm the only one still here."

"That answers my first question."

"Sorry I was tied up earlier. I got your message."

"Marilyn called you?" I asked without thinking.

"No. Ms. Kiefner told me you'd tried to get me. Who the hell is Marilyn?"

"Never mind."

"You don't sound so good, Owen."

"I don't look so good either. I've been to see a doctor."

"What's wrong?"

That question might have brought us back to Marilyn, but I stepped over her like a doubtful spot on the sidewalk. "Mildred Tucker shook me up some. The doctor I went to see was Robert Carteret's."

"Was?"

"Back when phone calls were a nickel." My '81 quarter was running out and I didn't know where to begin. "We have to talk, Harry."

"I'm late for a dinner meeting now."

"Robert Carteret can't remember what he had for dinner yesterday. He's been legally incompetent since the war. Maybe I should say, illegally incompetent.

Anyway, he didn't write our instructions." I waited a few seconds for an answer. "Say 'huh,' Harry, you'll feel better."

"Dad said he'd been wounded during the war."

"Harry, if you knew about this . . ."

"I didn't, Owen. Stay calm. My father wouldn't be associated with anything like that."

"Look, I don't have any more change. Can you call me back?"

"What's the number?"

I read it off and hung up with emphasis. Harry's dinner engagement had irritated me by contradicting the feeling I'd had that I was standing at the center of an important action. I stalled through the first two rings and picked up our conversation with an admission of defeat. "Are you going to be in tomorrow morning?"

"I can cancel tonight, Owen. I didn't mean to cut you off."

"It doesn't matter."

"What about your report?"

"I've already submitted it."

"I'm not following any of this." Harry's serious tone was an attempt to reestablish our professional relationship.

"I mean I've submitted a request for an extension. I'm pretty sure they'll go along."

"Would you mind starting at the beginning?"

"Carteret is a ward of his own company. His doctor wrote the famous letter. I don't know how it got as far as us. I fouled things up by directing attention back to Carteret himself." Inside the booth, my voice had an unfamiliar sound. I decided it was too much conviction. "I think that's what happened, anyway."

"Huh," Harry said. "How did you ask for an extension?"

"Using my own name."

"Damn it, Owen, that's not what I meant."

"Sorry. I've felt sort of detached today."

"I'm sorry about that myself," Harry said. "Why don't you call it a day. We'll talk first thing in the morning."

It sounded like a good plan. Harry had a talent for planning. He was a talented guy. He painted. He played the clarinet. In college he'd alternately planned to be an artist who played the clarinet and a musician who painted on the side. A lot of Harry's plans didn't work out.

SEVENTEEN

EVEN OVER THE PHONE, Harry had his usual cold shower effect. I'd gone into the hotel lobby the leader of a reckless expedition. I came out the victim of an irresponsible act. I felt like a child who had written on the living room wall. There was no hope of my action being overlooked or talked away. As a side effect of my deflation, I was tired. I wanted my bed, but my bachelor's survival instinct told me to eat something first.

I saw the long green awning of a restaurant a block to the east and headed that way. My expense account had disappeared at five, but disaster made me capricious. I stepped down from street level into comparative darkness and quiet. A curving, pink-lit bar lined the entryway.

The bar and its stools were padded with worn red vinyl that allowed me to date the place like an archaeologist. I decided that my narrow tie was right in period.

A bartender with a bow tie nodded in greeting. "What'd'ya know?" he asked.

"Scotch," I said.

I carried my drink with me into the interior. The place became darker as I walked, until I arrived at a small music stand lit by a brass lamp and the smile of the stout gentleman behind it. He picked up a menu without speaking and led me past half a dozen empty tables to one that must somehow have suited me.

"Thank you," I said.

I sipped my scotch and thought of how long the day had been. My nightcap worries about Agatha Christie and motiveless, passionless crimes seemed remote and absurd. In terms of fictional models, I'd somehow gone from the England of the thirties with its manor houses and manicured lawns to the scorched grass and bungalows of Southern California. World War II was a fresh wound, and the manipulation of wealth was the great evil. It won't buy you happiness, Sweetheart.

A waitress finally gave me an audience. Her snappy opening was a short cough and a pen poised above her pad.

"Guns don't kill, corporations do," I said.

"Tonight's vegetables are peas," she replied.

"And?"

"Peas."

"Thank you." I ordered the meat loaf, and she went away. I thought about another drink, but the intimate lighting of the room was already working on me. To keep my eyes open, I tried to decide if I'd been kidding Harry or myself on the phone. I asked myself if a corporate consciousness, even of 1950 vintage, could swallow a sick man whole. I asked myself how much momentum or vitality or desire to survive a paper entity could develop. No and none, I answered.

My answers were punctuated by the arrival of a Jell-O salad. I poked at it and explored corollaries. I could avoid my distaste for an impersonal solution by seizing on Carl Vernia, empire builder, but that was avoiding a tougher question. Dr. Schiel had posed it for me: Why would anyone be allowed to research William Carteret's death if Robert Carteret were a secret invalid? To that, I added another question, a personal one I could feel swimming around in the scotch in my stomach: Why me?

I HEARD THE PHONE in my apartment from half a flight away. I ran as far as the door before I convinced myself that it wasn't Marilyn. I locked the door behind me and crossed the room in the dark, knocking weekend dishes from an unseen coffee table. A woman's voice answered my hello.

"Owen Keane?"

"Yes," I said.

"This is Carolyn Vernia. I'd like to talk with you. I'm at my office in the Carteret Building. The guard will show you up."

I stood in the darkness for a long moment, like a startled sleeper trying to make sense of a dream. I had no way to reach Harry, and I couldn't think of anyone else who would give a damn. I thought of soaping a message on my bathroom mirror, to whom it may concern, and laughed aloud in the darkness. It wasn't my best laugh.

I turned on the lights long enough to find the two photographs I'd borrowed from Lois Parnell. I'd need them if I worked up enough nerve to carry out my bid for an extension. I was counting on Carolyn Vernia knowing little more of the business than I did. Dr. Schiel had described Carl Vernia as taciturn, and he had died suddenly.

Harry once commented that New York City was no place for a man with my depth of paranoia. My unstated answer was that a deep enough paranoia pales anything, even New York. I was reminded of that as I left my apartment. It was later than I liked to ride the subway, but I wasn't worried. I felt protected during my ride and on the street afterward by the idea that arriving safely was the worst thing that could happen to me.

I couldn't find a service bell at the Carteret Building, so I reached through the bars of the bronze screen, and tapped on the glass with my keys. The guard who answered was the slow, smiling former something I'd met earlier. Watching him walk across the lobby, I decided that he had been a soldier. His short gray hair was oiled in place, and he was getting fat. His fat had been muscle once, though, and it still looked hard enough to pass.

"Good evening, Mr. Keane," he said. "I hope you won't mind a pat-down."

We both smiled at the idea, but he searched me anyway. His partner watched the proceedings from his post by the elevators and then held one open for our ascent.

"Don't fall asleep, George," the first guard said.

I was picturing John Hyatt's sixth floor until the doors opened. Eleven looked like a different building. The lighting was dim, but I could see several large tapestries on distant walls, wrinkled and woven in dark reds and blues. Directly before us in the center of the entryway a tall, thin pedestal held a swirl of clear glass. It seemed to catch and hold what light there was.

"Think that's a horse?" the guard asked me. "I've always thought that's a horse's head."

We crossed deep beige carpet to a pair of tall glass doors, then stopped to look back.

"It's a fish," I said.

The approach to Carolyn Vernia was protected by low wooden work stations and potted plants arranged symmetrically on either side of the wide hallway. I was surprised when we made an asymmetrical turn to our left. Her office was well lit and open before us.

We stood on the threshold of the room, but the woman I'd come to see was still some distance away. They'd carved out a cavern in the old building to make her office, or so I guessed from an exposed girder that curved from the exterior wall to the high ceiling. The girder was massive and an incongruous beige, like everything else, and it functioned as a divider of sorts. On my side, a small table with four chairs stood away from the walls, an island in the plush carpet. Her desk was similarly centered on the far side of the room. It was small and backed by a large bookcase. The exterior wall was cut by half a dozen windows, which were narrow by current standards and effectively blocked by the skyscraper next door.

Carolyn Vernia looked up from her reading after a moment. "Thank you, Miller," she said.

My friend the guard turned and left me without a word. I didn't expect him to go too far. I began across the room without an invitation. It was a long trip. She waited patiently until I was stopped short of her desk by a perimeter of visitors' chairs.

"You're not what I expected," she said. It had been the theme of my day. As I'd guessed from her photograph, she was a small woman. Because of that, her face seemed unusually broad. It was also too young and unmarked for the hairstyle that framed it. Her large brown eyes were making their own appraisal. "You're a little thin for a detective."

"I'm not a detective," I said.

"You're not? Are you sure? I'll be very disappointed if that's true. I'm an old fan of detective stories. Not mystery stories per se. I mean ones with a good, solid, fifty-a-day-plus-expenses detective. Philip Marlowe, Lew Archer. Do you understand the distinction?''

"Yes," I said.

"I'm afraid I read quite a few of them when I was younger." She spoke slowly and deliberately, as if to tell me that her roundabout opening wasn't a sign of nervousness. "Now I don't have time for even that innocent bad habit." She gestured toward the reports on her desk. "What do you know about EFTS, Mr. Keane?"

"Nothing."

"It stands for Electronic Funds Transfer System. You'll be hearing a lot about it over the next few years, I'm afraid. Teller machines, debit cards, and the like. I suppose I should have wasted my youth on science fiction. I'd be more enthusiastic about paperless banking if I thought it would cut down on these damn reports." She pulled my blank report from beneath the pile and flipped through it. "Your effort was a refreshing change of pace from these," she said. "Like you, though, a little thin. I'm afraid you'll never compete with Ross Macdonald, Mr. Keane. This doesn't have much of an ending."

"It's the latest thing in detective stories. You write your own ending." I noted with relief that my voice wasn't quivering.

"Your dialogue sounds promising, but you're still below the mark physically."

"Sorry."

"You'd find it a handicap, if you were a detective. I mean, I can't imagine women offering themselves to you on short notice."

Or long acquaintance, I thought, but there was no point in ganging up on myself. "It saves me from having to dodge the older ones," I said.

She laughed at that. "Very good. If you loosen your tie, you might actually carry it off."

"Look, Ms. Vernia..."

"Miss."

"Do you mind if I sit down?" My left knee had begun to twitch so strongly that I felt it must be obvious to her. My body was becoming a loose assortment of barely controllable nervous reactions. I took her silence for permission and picked the closest chair. My clothes felt moist and warm against its cool leather.

"I'm not Humphrey Bogart," I said. "I'm not tough. I feel silly when I try to be. Right now I'm pretty close to asking for a drink of water. If we could just talk about Robert Carteret, I'd really appreciate it."

Her brown eyes watched me without revealing anything of the woman within. "I'm tough," she said. "Do you believe that?"

"Yes."

She tapped the cover of my report. "What is this all about?"

"Grandstand play. I wanted to talk with you."

"You could have made an appointment."

"And gotten such service?"

Her expression suggested that even my patter was failing. "You're taking a very great risk, I hope you realize that. If there is the least suggestion of blackmail, I'll show you service you'll never forget."

"I was working for your boss."

"Your firm was. This doesn't appear to be a business communication."

"Just avoiding publicity. I didn't think you'd want any."

"You seem to think this company is guilty of some crime."

"It doesn't have to be illegal to be embarrassing."

Her answer to that was a piece of typing paper. She held it close to her nose and read. "Robert Carteret was wounded in action in Italy on January 26, 1944, while serving with the Third Infantry Division of the U.S. 6th Corps. He was awarded both the Purple Heart and the Silver Star. His wounds resulted in permanent disability. Because of this, and because he is the last of his family line, Mr. Carteret created a trust, which took effect on April 23, 1947, to manage his estate until the time of his death. He has since devoted himself to charitable works."

Copy the *Times*, the *News*, and the *Post*, I thought.

"Well?" she asked.

"A little wordy."

"You're disappointing me, Mr. Keane. I expected better, after the reports I've had. Let me see. I've heard you are a man of integrity but lacking focus. That your mind tends to wander dangerously when it is without occupation. And that you're loyal. I've even heard that you'd studied for the priesthood. Is that true?"

She hadn't had time for elaborate research. I took a chance on an alternative I didn't like. "When did you call Mr. Ohlman?"

I liked her answer even less. "I didn't call him, he called me, and not very long after your report arrived. He was afraid you'd done something impulsive. He also said you are impulsive, incidentally. If it's any consolation, I think he was trying to protect you."

From myself, of course. "You said you had reports."

"Yes. I also heard from Donald Schiel. My afternoon was very busy toward the end. He warned me that you might be headed my way. That's how I happened to be waiting around after business hours to receive your report. He said you were determined to represent Robert Carteret, even though he's a totally disinterested party. And that you seemed to have some secret motivation. You can understand why I wanted to meet you. I was sure you were a detective."

"Sorry again."

"Dr. Schiel also wanted to tell me something I already knew, to confess it, actually."

"That he wrote the Carteret letter."

"Correct," she said, displaying her initial irritation. I had to do more than steal her punch lines if I hoped to accomplish my purpose. I needed time. Not to reconcile myself to what she'd just told me. That would take more than time. I felt wronged and sorry for myself. And I was tired. My nervous energy seemed to have run out through my twitching kneecap. I felt again like a truant child: The world was a conspiracy of people who knew more than I did, even about myself. I needed time to use the trick of a child, to escape an unpleasant reality through a bold statement of imagination. While I watched for an opening, I fell back on the routine of question and answer.

"Did Dr. Schiel ask you why you had permitted an investigation?"

"He told me your opinion. On this point, it happens to be correct. I am curious about the Carterets.

Believe it or not, I'm too young to remember when William Carteret was alive. I grew up fascinated by the little bit of their story I knew. When I started at the bank there were plenty of people around who had known both William and Robert. And their father, too. I was able to fill in a lot of the family history. Except, of course, the part no one knows, the business of William Carteret's death.''

That she had agreed with my idea seemed to discredit it. I reached for another reason, something beneath the surface. "Did you ever ask your own father?''

"No.'' She paused in search of an explanation. "He didn't like to speak of that time.''

"He saw William on the morning of his death.''

She took my first trump easily. "Along with half the bank, if you believe the stories. They were having a board meeting, or at least they tried to. William broke it up early and went to fly off in the wrong direction.''

"Why didn't your father like to discuss Carteret's death?''

"I'm beginning to feel as though I'm being questioned, Mr. Keane.''

"Force of habit,'' I said.

"I don't know why my father should be brought into this.''

"It's a detective story, remember?''

She picked up my report and read aloud again. "Which Carteret brother are you holding on Long Island?'' She let the report fall noisily on the leather top of her desk. "Explain that.''

My hand was forced, but she'd set the scene more effectively than I could have done. I produced my borrowed photographs and laid them on the desk before her. "Pick Robert Carteret."

She lowered her broad face and studied the photographs for several minutes. "They were brothers," she finally said.

"I know. Born two years apart. The resemblance isn't miraculous, just interesting. Like the second son of a New York banker becoming a private in the infantry."

"Robert was drafted, and his father was dead."

"His father's bank was still alive and being run by the firstborn."

"There was bad blood between the brothers," she conceded. "Over a girl."

"The same girl who died in the plane crash, as you know."

"Yes," she said with an impatient nod. "Lynn Baxter."

I indicated one of the photographs with a hand that shook only slightly. "She's the one with the braids."

She went down for another look and came up unimpressed.

I moved on, without giving her time to reflect. "Which brings us to the most interesting part of the story. To get to Albany from Long Island, William flew south."

"He changed his mind."

"Maybe. Maybe Lynn Baxter changed hers."

"Switched her affections to Robert?"

"Back to Robert. He'd been the first Carteret in her life." She looked surprised at that, which I took as a good sign. "He'd also become the disenfranchised son, about to march off to war. Lynn Baxter was a romantic girl, from what I've been told. Robert could fly the *Phaeton*. That's what William called his plane. You remember Phaeton, Miss Vernia. He borrowed the sun god's chariot but couldn't handle it.''

"How does subsituting Robert for William explain flying south?''

"Their time was short. Her mother was a social climber with designs on William. Lynn and Robert couldn't marry in New York without a dangerous delay. But they could in Maryland.''

My audience shifted her gaze to a point directly above my head. Until she spoke, I thought it was a sign of impatience. "Robert reported for duty on October 15, 1941,'' she said.

"Or William did. Five days after the crash. The full-scale search hadn't even begun. When the bodies were finally found in July, he was probably overseas.''

"Someone surely saw him in five days' time.''

"It would be tough to find out. During the war, your father closed the house and scattered the help.''

"Why would William take Robert's place in the army?''

"The old gossip against Robert had him reporting for duty to avoid the responsibility for two murders. Switch the names.''

"That was just gossip.''

"The Civil Aeronautics Board report on the crash cited a massive loss of engine oil. It could have been the result of a mechanical failure or a careless mistake or something else. I've talked with the man who worked on the *Phaeton*. He voted for something else.''

Carolyn Vernia, bank president, sat before me, tough but indecisive. Like me, she was a victim of bad reading. Like most of us, she was a prisoner of her own limited experience of life. "Go on,'' she said.

"The rest is easy. William is wounded at Anzio. When he wakes up, everybody tells him that he's Robert Carteret. If he knows better, he keeps his mouth shut. His prewar memory is in pieces. What he can recall could apply to either brother. There's a good chance that he no longer knew his real name. Dr. Schiel thinks Carteret's illness is as much emotional as physical. That he shut out all his pain at once. Including the pain of having killed his brother and the woman he loved."

I thought I might have been working too hard, but her expression was still uncritical. Her last objection was halfhearted. "They weren't identical twins. My father would have recognized William."

"Funny how your father keeps popping up. Dr. Schiel told me another funny thing. In all his visits to the estate, he never saw a photograph of William." It was the kind of detail that means nothing in a court of law and everything in a paperback. The kind of clue Carolyn Vernia and I had both believed in, once upon a time.

Her silent attention was a considerable temptation, but I decided to stop. My best play was to give her a framework to fill in. I retrieved the photographs and stood up. It was easier than sitting down had been.

"Where are you going?" she asked me.

"I'm not sure yet," I said, answering the larger question.

"I haven't decided what to do with you." She made it sound like a serious problem.

"You and Harry can talk it over, now that you're acquainted. Buy him a drink, and he'll tell you about the good old days when I dated his wife." I delivered my speech backing away from the desk. It covered me as far as the overhanging girder. I felt its weight above me as I waited for a reply.

She considered me with the same serious look for a moment, then looked down at my report. I was dismissed.

EIGHTEEN

MILLER WAS WAITING for me near the glass sea horse. He punched the down button of the elevator call without saying a word. His earlier smile was gone, and I wondered if I'd kept him past his shift. I played with that small deduction, because Carolyn Vernia had told me things I didn't want to think about.

"You through for the night?" I asked.

"One more job," Miller said.

When the elevator arrived, Miller held the door for me and took his place at the controls. I watched him jab the button for the first floor before I lost interest. I began to think of my current position, almost against my will. It wasn't a pleasant occupation, so I examined the elevator instead. Like the floor I'd just left, the car was more modern than its building. The quality carpeting ran up the walls for a foot or two, meeting Formica-like panels. The ceiling was mirrored. My foreshortened reflection looked down at me with tired eyes. I watched the eyes open wider as the elevator came to a sudden, hard stop.

The floor indicator said five, but the doors didn't open. The red knob marked "Emergency Stop" had been pulled out. Miller was standing with his hands behind his back, examining the mirrored ceiling. Watching me impersonally in the personal space of the elevator.

I looked from the doors to the Formica panels. I was more confined than on the subway and more exposed than on a street corner. I took a meaningless step away from Miller and turned to face him. His oily gray hair looked metallic in the elevator's bright light. I used the difference in our ages to calculate my chances of defending myself. I decided I didn't have a prayer.

"What's up?" I asked.

His nonchalance was equally awkward. "I've been told that these mirrored ceilings are to give visitors one last chance to preen before they present themselves," he said. "Salesmen and customers both. But you can't really see too much, can you?"

"No," I said, hoping that it was true.

"Couldn't tell if you'd lost a button, or anything personal."

"What's the point?" I asked.

"Small talk," Miller said. He looked down from the mirror to me.

"Can you start this thing?" I asked.

"In a little while."

"George is going to be worried."

Miller smiled at that. "George will be anything I tell him to be."

It looked as though Miller would ramble all night if I kept feeding him straight lines. I decided to keep my mouth shut until he got down to business. He stared at me long enough to achieve some mysterious purpose before beginning.

"I'm the supervisor of uniform security for the corporation," he said. "It was only a coincidence that I was downstairs this afternoon. I stayed this evening because I thought your business required a personal touch."

I looked at his hands involuntarily. His personal touch didn't promise to be a soft one.

"I listened in on your conversation with Miss Vernia," he said. "I didn't like the idea of her being in there alone with you. She's pretty tough, and you look harmless enough, but I didn't like it. I didn't catch what you were selling her, but I heard Miss Vernia say that you're representing Robert Carteret. Is that true?"

"It was," I said. "I'm not representing anyone now, and I'm not trying to shake anybody down, if that's what you're worried about."

He considered the idea briefly with a small smile before returning to his line of march. "I knew Robert. I've worked for the corporation since 1960. My first assignment was at the Carteret estate."

I decided that he didn't intend to threaten me physically, but without that idea I was disoriented. And I was tired of the Carterets. "Why are you telling me this?" I asked.

"You mentioned a shakedown. I want to tell you about a real shakedown. At least I think it was real. I always figured that it had something to do with the death of Robert's brother. I never knew any of the details, which means they weren't around to know. But I had a hard time believing that Robert could have been involved. A decorated infantryman and all. You're the first one to stand up for him. That's why I'm backing you."

Carolyn Vernia's barn of an office must have hampered Miller's eavesdropping. If he had heard my side of the conversation, he'd have serious doubts about my loyalty to his war hero. "I may be more trouble than help," I said. "And I don't think I'm working for the corporation anymore."

"Trouble doesn't worry me," Miller replied. "William Carteret isn't the only skeleton in the corporation's closet. He's just the only one I don't understand."

"I meant I may be finished with this business."

"I don't think so," Miller said. "I don't think this business is finished with you." He paused to let me consider that before starting in. "Have you ever heard of Peter Gregson?"

"Over and over again. He was the Carteret grounds keeper. He was the last person to see the Carteret plane in the air."

"By the time I met him, he was lucky if he could see his feet. Or use them. He was a drunk and a nasty one."

"And you didn't like him."

Miller actually seemed surprised. "No," he said. "No one did. He was a nasty little guy, like I said. Drunk at any hour when he wasn't asleep. Used the trees of the estate like a dog would. Wandered the whole place like he owned it. He had a rough mouth, too. He was offensive to the women and disrespectful to Robert. Not physically rough. We wouldn't have stood for that. But he'd laugh at him sometimes, taunt him."

"Why did you let him get away with it?"

"That's what I'd like to know. I mean, I know we were ordered to do it. I'd like to know what was behind the order."

"You think Gregson was blackmailing the corporation?"

"You tell me. He lived over the old carriage house, rent free. They called it a carriage house anyway, but it was really just a big garage. He was retired when I hired on in '60, but even the old hands couldn't remember him ever pulling a weed.

"I was sent on booze runs for him, if he spilled too much and ran short." That memory bothered Miller more than any of Gregson's other offenses. "He died one weekend while I was on leave. When I got back he was in the ground, and all of his things were gone."

"Gone?"

"Thrown away. The carriage-house loft hasn't been used in the eighteen years since."

"How did he die?"

"Booze. He was dying the three years I knew him. If he'd had any family they might have dried him out. We just bought him more booze every time he snapped his fingers.

"One night it was raining when he ran out. I was the junior man on duty, so I got wet. I had car trouble, too. I was in a black mood when I got to that sty of a loft, and Gregson made it worse. What took me so long, he wanted to know. I was mad enough to ask him what he'd done with his morning bottle. He laughed at me. He'd spilled it, he said. All of that liquor had run out through the knothole next to my flat feet, he said, because there wasn't as much as a throw rug to sop it up. But it was a magic hole, he told me. Booze came out of it. He picked up the bottle I'd brought him. Here's some now, he said. Whiskey from the magic hole. And all because the son of a bitch who owned the place hadn't seen fit to buy him a scrap of rug. Now he was too sentimental to cover it up, he said. He opened the bottle and took the first slug right there. Then he bowed from the waist and thanked the hole in the floor.

"I told him he was crazy and left. He called down the stairs after me, telling me I should listen to knotholes. I might hear the voice of the dead."

NINETEEN

OWEN KEANE SLEPT with the phone off the hook, rose early, and walked three blocks to the small garage where he stored his car. Despite the early hour, the corner lot on which the garage stood was the scene of much noisy activity. Three cars formed a line at the single ancient gas pump, their drivers leaning from open windows to discuss a ball game. A small utility truck was being backed into a bay of the garage, an operation that was aided by the combined lung power of four hangers-on. Keane made his way across the oily sidewalk and the still oilier black-top yard and entered the garage office. Manny, the owner, was on the phone, discussing the complications that would attend an upcoming ring job. Without interrupting his description, he swiveled his chair to retrieve a set of keys from a cabinet behind his desk. He tossed the keys to Keane, his hand finishing up in a friendly wave.

I saw myself that morning as a character in a story. Someone else's story. In addition to a detached perspective, the idea gave me a fatalistic attitude. Wherever I wandered, I felt, the plot would follow me. Wandering was a big priority for me that morning. Also getting away and being somewhere else. So I'd gone in search of my old Volkswagen, my '65 Karmann-Ghia.

I found the car where I'd left it, in the back of Manny's lot parked between two domestic junkers.

The Ghia looked pretty good in comparison. Although it was mechanically identical to a Beetle, the little car had lower, rounder lines. Fifties lines. A poor man's Porsche, the guy who sold it to me had called it. Mine had the standard rot around the headlights and a hole or two in the rocker panels. The red paint was a little chalky and the chrome was covered with tiny brown bumps that looked like drying poison ivy. Nothing too bad. I brushed a few dead leaves from the base of the windshield and climbed in. When I turned the key, a faint clicking arose from the engine compartment. On the second try, the engine turned over slowly. It caught on the third attempt, and I was off in a cloud of blue smoke.

I made my way south to the Belt Parkway and followed it to the Verrazano Bridge. I then wandered across unloved Staten Island, finally leaving the city on the Goethals Bridge across the Arthur Kill. On the Jersey side, I traveled an elevated highway past miles of old docks and factory buildings that edged oily marshland. Eventually, the old decay was replaced by the huge tanks and mad pipework of oil refineries. The pipes sent an old shudder through me, the fear of a fabric so complex that no one could see the whole or understand more than the smallest part. I was relieved to finally spot the Garden State Parkway. I headed south along the Jersey shore.

My tentative destination was a town with the informal name of Toms River. From a faded map I'd found in the Ghia's glove box, I'd learned that Toms River was the seat of Ocean County, the county where the *Phaeton* had made its last landing. I was hoping to find one more clue there among the local records, the clue that would tip the balance my way. That was my plan, but when I was still a few miles short of Toms River I left the Parkway and drove east to the ocean instead.

I parked the Ghia at Seaside Heights, a town I'd tried to know on summer nights years before. The whole place was being mothballed now against the approaching winter, boarded up, packed away, or tied down. What remained in view looked tired and cheap. An October morning was the wrong time for the place. It needed a summer night in mid-July, with a warm breeze coming off the ocean and a thousand kids on the boardwalk, all looking for something. Looking in an inexperienced way and in a place that made their looking hopeless. Instead of getting on to Toms River, I walked the boardwalk. I felt again like one of those searching children, and I wanted to have one more look, for luck. I had long since learned that I wouldn't find what I wanted at the beach, but I looked there anyway. The light was better.

I walked south on the weathered boards, counting and recounting my emotional change. I still felt a physical ache in my chest at the thought of Harry selling me out to Carolyn Vernia by telling her that, however I represented myself, I was and always would be a failed priest. The wound left by that failure was still fresh enough to make me start in pain when someone touched it. That was because I hadn't simply changed my mind about my vocation. I had been found wanting. I was a paratrooper who had frozen at the doorway of the plane, unable to jump. I'd failed to cross the void of doubt in the only way it could be crossed—or so I'd been told—in a single, unreflecting leap. I'd chosen instead to wander through the darkness on foot, unguided except for the clues I stumbled across, the little mysteries I solved.

The one or two people I now passed on my walk eyed me strangely. They might have recognized, as Harry and Marilyn and Dr. Schiel had, that I was somehow outside their world looking in. Then again, it may just have been that I was strolling along the boardwalk in a suit and tie.

Above me, rows of dark gray clouds were sailing by like impossible fleets. The beach was all but empty. On my right, the concession stands gave way to ugly Gothic beach houses that fronted for hundreds of smaller ones that were less fortunately placed. They looked deserted, too. No endless blue sky, no sun, no million-dollar retreats clinging to wave-washed cliffs. The ocean was even on the wrong side. It was enough to disorient any paperback detective. A detective would have been tailing someone or waiting to tail someone or calling a cooperative friend on the force to ask for a check on the last three digits of a license plate. None of my secondhand training seemed to apply. I'd come to the scene of the crime with a purpose but without the heart to follow it through. Dr. Schiel had told Carolyn Vernia that I had a secret motivation for pursuing the Carteret mystery. At the moment it was a secret even from me.

My motive for fleeing the city was easier to identify. I'd wanted to escape Harry's lecture and subsequent apology, and I'd felt my time running out. If Carolyn Vernia hadn't already punched holes in my plot, she soon would. I'd depended, during our interview, on her knowing little of her father's part in the affair. That strategy had worked temporarily, but I'd left too many loose ends strewn about her office. I'd also left her with the desire to follow them up. Beyond that, the reasons for my sudden urge to travel grew vague. Somehow, Robert Carteret's problem had become my own. Harry might have called it the moment in the story when the detective fights to clear himself of a murder he didn't commit. I think I was fighting to clear myself of a reality I hadn't committed, but fighting may be too strong a word.

Dr. Schiel told me he'd written the letter I still carried to answer the one question that would give Robert Carteret peace. That was an impossible task, of course. There was no peace for a man who couldn't remember an answer if he were given it, a man who could only remember the feel of the question. But the letter touched other questions for other people, and that explained its existence and continued life. For Schiel, the question concerned the one professional lapse that compromised a promising career. For Carolyn Vernia, the mystery of a father. And for Owen Keane, what? What was I after?

I asked myself that question as my walk carried me into a new town: Seaside Park. Here the boardwalk ended, giving way to an ordinary, if sandy, sidewalk. The houses that fronted the beach road were also ordinary, middle-American fare. Large but undistinguished, the houses could have been—like the families who rented them each summer—refugees from any number of identical inland towns.

I had one house in particular in mind as the goal of my walk, my apparently meandering approach just being my way of sneaking up on myself. I almost walked past the place before I recognized it. It was three stories high and shingled, with graying white paint, a deep front porch, and an aura of association.

I'd spent a week in the old house once, the week I'd foolishly told Marilyn about one evening in a theater lounge, the week of the summer retreat when I'd met Jimmy, the boy who had been spoken to by God.

I'd also met my Moriarty that week, the archenemy that still confounded me. Unfortunately for me, my enemy was not a person who could be tossed into a convenient waterfall. It was an idea, the idea that the universe is godless and capricious, without pattern or meaning. I had faced my frightening enemy steadfastly on that first encounter, with a courage that now made me feel both foolish and proud as I recalled it.

Standing before the old house, I tried to focus on the feeling of pride. It seemed to answer my earlier questions about my motivation. The Carterets mattered to me because my Moriarty still mattered, because I had never been able to simply accept the pointlessness around me and go on, as Harry and Marilyn and countless others had. I'd tried to fill the emptiness with profitable nine-to-five pursuits, with interests and hobbies and people. I'd almost made it work. Even now, a stray thought of Marilyn and all the possibilities she represented could fill me with doubt and regret. But still I'd come back to this first place, this shrine sacred only to me, to renew my vow.

I started back to find my car with a more resolute step, remembering how I'd once marched off up this same street determined to solve mysteries. My goals were more modest now. I was only determined to keep trying.

TWENTY

THE OCEAN COUNTY Courthouse was a large, pseudocolonial building with grass still brown from the summer heat and a large American flag that sounded plastic in the steady breeze. The building was flanked by a three-shed fire station on the left and a blacktop lot on the right. The lot contained half a dozen idle police cars, suggesting that the off-season for the Jersey shore extended at least this far inland. The sheriff's offices looked new and worn at the same time. I stopped at a counter that came up to my chest. I thought immediately of a New York Public Library counter but shook off the association.

A man in his forties wearing a brown-and-tan uniform and a silver star looked up from his newspaper. If he was at the right desk, he was Deputy Robert Hinkle. "Help you?" he asked.

"I'm trying to find some information on a plane crash that occurred near Smithtown on October 10, 1941," I began.

Hinkle interrupted me. "You're twenty-three years too late." He spoke with more North Jersey than I'd expected, and he punctuated his remark with an incongruous horselaugh. "Sorry, but the original courthouse and all the records were lost in a big fire in 1958."

I had an irrational mental picture of Carl Vernia holding a torch. "Is there anyone around who was working back then?" I asked.

"Yeah, but they're all dead." Another laugh. "Sorry, buddy. I'm the veteran of the force, and I've only lived down here since '61. Used to live in Bayonne, but they were ready to condemn the whole joint."

"Do you know Smithtown?"

Hinkle wheeled his chair a foot to the left and pointed to a map of the county that was pinned to the wall. "There it is. Down south of here on Five Thirty-nine. Almost to the county line. Yeah, I know Smithtown. Probably named after the only guy who lives there. No kidding, it's no more than a defunct filling station and a vegetable stand. You'll be lucky if anybody there remembers what happened last week, never mind 1941."

"Thanks," I said, feeling my small store of determination begin to dwindle.

"Pineys, probably," Hinkle was saying. "That's all that lives back in there. They're worse than hillbillies. Crazy idiots from inbreeding, you know. First-cousin marriages and worse. They'd as soon shoot you as say hello."

"Thanks a lot." I was already thinking that my trip to Toms River was officially a failure. Then Deputy Hinkle came through for me.

"If I were you," he said, "I'd check with the *Sunbeam*. That's our county weekly." He held up his newspaper to display the masthead. "Published since the turn of the century. Talk to Tim Gleason, he's the editor. Nice guy, when he isn't stoned."

I found the *Sunbeam* offices in a corner storefront that might once have held a drugstore. The small city room was clean and modern. Too clean, in fact, and too quiet. If the *Sunbeam* was any indication, the world was on hold until Memorial Day.

"Anybody here?" I asked aloud. As if in response, a phone in the corner of the room began to ring. A door to my left opened and a young man in jeans and a T-shirt came out, carrying a coffee cup. Halfway to the phone, he noticed me.

"Be right with you." He walked to the phone and answered it with the name of the paper. During the long silence that followed, his head bobbed up and down, moving to the rhythm of a voice I couldn't hear. From time to time his eyes would roll to the ceiling. "Broken, huh?" he finally said. "That's too bad. Look, I'll send somebody right over." His head kept time for another measure. "Right. Tell you what, I'll probably come over myself. How's that? Okay. Bye." He had a long thin face and large blue eyes that almost dominated a long nose. The nose looked familiar. I decided that it was not unlike my own. He noticed the resemblance as he crossed the room.

"I should warn you right off, I don't believe in nepotism."

"I don't think we're related," I said.

"Then we're wasting a lot of homely. I'm Tim Gleason."

I introduced myself, and he led me back to the only desk in the room that was cluttered. "Seems we've had a disaster at the bird sanctuary," Gleason said. "Sparrow hawk breaks wing. Bad for the bird, but lucky for the *Sunbeam.* I was afraid I'd have to run the milk ads on the front page. Can I get you some coffee?"

"No thanks," I said.

He tasted his. "Sound decision. I had to make it myself. My full-time staff is out having her lunch. We're not that small really, but we're slow today, even for the start of the off-season. We take two or three interns on in the summer, believe it or not, and the place really hums. So what have you got for me?"

The question suggested a problem I'd considered on the short drive from the sheriff's office: a newspaperman might see a story in my questions about the Carteret crash. I didn't want publicity any more than Carolyn Vernia did. In spite of my lousy track record, I fell back on fabrication. I'd decided that Gleason might respect another journalist's right to an exclusive more than he would an invalid's right to privacy.

"I'm hoping you can help me," I began. "I work in a law office in New York, but I'm trying to break into free-lance writing. I've taken some courses at night, but so far I haven't had much luck." Gleason's blue eyes showed empathy, and the first, thin glaze of boredom. "I think I've come across an idea for a story that will really sell."

"Uh-huh," Gleason said.

"It has to do with a playboy aviator named William Carteret. Have you heard of him?"

"No," Gleason said.

"His family owned a bank in New York, Carteret Federal. I'm sure you've heard of that. The bank's still owned and operated by the same family, which gives the whole thing currency." Gleason smiled at my unconscious pun, and I threw in my last reserves of enthusiasm.

"Carteret died in a crash near Smithtown, New Jersey, on October 10, 1941." I paused for an effect that no longer impressed me. "He was on a flight from

Long Island to Albany. To this day, no one knows why he flew south.''

Gleason the journalist's smile became a conspiratorial grin. ''Sounds like a winner,'' he said.

''I've come down to look into the crash investigation. There's something odd about that, too. The plane wasn't found for nine months.''

Gleason laughed at that. ''Odd? They're lucky they found it at all. Smithtown, right? Hell, that's way back in the Barrens. You know about the Pine Barrens, don't you?''

''I've driven through pine forests down here.''

''On the way to the beach, right? You and ten million other people. Most don't know a thing about the place. There's your free-lance article. I'd write a book about it, but John McPhee beat me to it. I've got a copy of his book here somewhere.'' He opened and closed a couple of drawers in a perfunctory way. ''Anyway, you should read it. New Jersey is the most densely populated state in the union. More than a thousand people per square mile, average. The Pines average less than fifteen. More than six hundred thousand acres of pine trees and bogs less than three hours' drive from your New York office.''

I broke in at that point to remind him of our first topic. ''I may be able to use it in my story.'' It didn't work.

''I'm giving you a better story,'' Gleason said. ''There's a fight going on around the Pines that should be making headlines in New York. I've sent stories to the *Times,* but if they don't need copy for the New Jersey section, they're not interested.''

Gleason pushed his chair back and put his sneakers on the desk. His rapid delivery suggested that his subject was well rehearsed. "The story really starts with the groundwater," he said. "An untapped aquifer bigger than anything on the East Coast. No kidding, the sand of the Pines soaks up water like a sponge. It boggles the mind. You've got all this pure water draining off into the Atlantic, and fifty miles away Philadelphia is dying for a clean drink. That alone would be a story.

"But there's a better angle. We've got casino gambling in Atlantic City now. Big boom for South Jersey. It's great for the economy, but bad for the aquifer. Sand doesn't filter worth a damn. Too much progress, too much sewage, too much dumping, and the aquifer could be polluted.

"New Jersey is supposed to be dead environmentally, but it's a bread-and-butter issue here, let me tell you. The governor's put a moratorium on building in the Pines. I wrote an editorial in support of it. Real fiery stuff. I've got a copy of it around here somewhere. Anyway, a lot of people are mad. They want the boom. They want the building and the money that comes with it, and to hell with the water and air. And then there are people who are saying, 'enough.' Let them get rich spoiling Nevada or Utah or wherever, but leave New Jersey alone."

I almost said "enough" myself. Instead I asked: "How do the Pineys feel about it?"

For the first time, Gleason paused to think. "It's mixed from what I can see," he said. "Some of them still live off the land and don't want it touched. But a lot of them want the work. Some of them are builders."

He waved a long-fingered hand to signal a turn in the conversation. "They don't like to be called 'Piney,' incidentally. Not by an outsider. You might remember that if you ever meet one.''

"You should mention that to Deputy Hinkle," I said.

"Hinkle's just worked his way up to 'Afro-American.' A real credit to the community, that guy. You've been to see Hinkle, huh?''

"The Ocean County Sheriff's Office helped to identify Carteret's body. I thought I might look through their records, but they were lost in a fire.''

"Courthouse fire of 1958.''

"Yes.''

Gleason tapped the side of his head. "Sometimes I amaze myself," he said. "You might try the state police in Trenton.''

"I was hoping you'd have something on it here.''

Gleason nodded. "Let's check the archives." He pushed himself away from the desk and swiveled the chair in one lazy motion. At the far end of the room, he opened a thin panel door that led to a walk-in closet. Gunmetal bookshelves held large bound volumes that looked like mismatched encyclopedias.

"Nineteen forty-one would be the *Sentinel* period." Gleason turned to me to explain. "This paper has published more or less continuously since 1889, but it's had half a dozen different names. It's only been the *Sunbeam* since the fifties. Personally, I'd like something more impressive, maybe *World Guardian*. Unfortunately, I'm only the editor. You said October '41?''

"The plane was found in July of '42.''

"Right. Here you go. You can use one of the desks.''

The volume he handed me was black and heavy. When I opened it, it gave off a musty odor. That physical presence impressed me more than the *Times* microfilm had. It made the *Sentinel* seem a more credible source. The front page stories were local echoes of the ones I'd read in the library the week before. Battles that were sweeping headlines in the *Times* had filtered down as stories of local boys killed and wounded. They were sadder stories for that, and I felt I knew why the paper had changed its name.

The articles describing the discovery of the plane also had a local slant. The first one was accompanied by a photograph taken at the crash site. It was heavily retouched and looked almost like a cartoon. The fuselage of the plane was still recognizable. I remembered a comment made by Gus Warden: Carteret had almost managed a safe landing.

Some of the details that had escaped the *Times* were insignificant, like the names of the deputies who had guarded the crash site. But the preliminary medical testimony contained in the local paper was more complete. Both occupants of the plane had died of head injuries, which I already knew. The *Sentinel* reported an interesting distinction: the woman's skull was "cracked," the man's was described as "crushed."

"You awake?" Gleason asked me. "The way you were staring off into 1942, I thought you might be asleep with your eyes open. You've got to watch that stuff. I knew people in college who went into libraries and never came out." He walked around to look over my shoulder. "Find anything?"

"One or two things. This story says the plane crashed near Hubbards Mill. Is that a mistake?"

"Sounds like a pine town. I've got an old map around here somewhere. There are a lot of ghost towns in the Pines. Some date from before the Revolutionary War. A local reporter wouldn't have worried about using a name like that to pinpoint the site. Not in 1942, anyway. The New York reporters said Smithtown because it was the closest thing on their auto club map. Smithtown is on Highway Five Thirty-nine, isn't it? That road really hummed before the Parkway was built. Just like today, people had no idea what they were driving through."

I looked around for the notebook I'd cleverly left in my apartment, and settled for my memory. "The official report of the crash said six miles south of Smithtown and nine miles east of Bargersville."

Gleason had found his map. He wrestled it open on an empty desk. "That sounds more like it," he said. There was a sudden flurry of long fingers around his head. "Wait a minute. Wait a minute. The Gleason brainpan is beginning to heat up. I'm going to do you a favor and a half." He pointed to the map. "Jim Skiles lives back in there. Skiles is a storyteller. It used to be a respected profession in the Pines. McPhee talks about it in his book. Anyway, Skiles is about seventy years old, and he lives back in the woods in a tar-paper shack. He's practically illiterate, so he keeps all his stories in his head. Oral tradition and that kind of stuff. He can tell you about things that happened in the Pines when he was five.

"I've been to see him a couple of times." Gleason spoke with some pride. "He doesn't really like outsiders. He wouldn't let me tape any of his stuff because he didn't want strangers to hear his stories. He likes to know a person first."

Gleason was clearly impressed by this simple creed. Our resemblance extended beyond our long noses, I decided. We were both surprised by the odd principle we came across.

"How can I find him?" I asked.

"I'll draw you a map. Tell him I sent you. And go easy on him, okay?" He paused to display his first serious expression.

"I won't ruin your groundwork," I said.

Gleason conveyed his satisfaction with a laugh. "Just remember that I've got an option on your story, if the *Times* turns you down. Stringing for us is a big responsibility. Keep the *Sunbeam* name pure!"

TWENTY-ONE

I TOOK HIGHWAY Five Thirty-one east from Toms River until it crossed Five Thirty-nine at a nameless intersection. Then I headed south once more, grinding my Volkswagen's tired gears as I went. I was paying more attention to the scenery than I was to my shifting. The pine trees I passed seemed both familiar and strange, like old friends seen for the first time in years. At first, with an occasional house or store set in the foreground, the dark green pines were the same boring scenery I'd watched fifteen years before on weekend drives to the beach. Farther south, the towns thinned out, and the trees became for me the awesome forest Tim Gleason had sketched.

The past glories of Five Thirty-nine were spoken of by roadside stands, weathered to the bare wood, the skeletal remains of billboards, overgrown by vines, and widely spaced filling stations, converted to other uses or standing empty. My last real landmark was Smithtown. Deputy Hinkle had been correct in his assessment of that bump in the road. The only sign of life I could see as I passed was a small group of dusty chickens pecking by the roadside.

The last part of Gleason's directions specified distances, and the Volkswagen's odometer was frozen nostalgically at thirty thousand miles. I used the speedometer and the second hand on my watch to judge the remaining distance. About five miles past Smithtown, I turned right onto an unpaved road. The

road was really a double track of sand divided by a
median of weeds and small bushes that scraped the
Ghia's flat bottom. The pine trees, close on either side,
reflected the noise of my motor, making it sound as
though I were being pursued by an angry lawn mower.
I stopped for a moment with the engine off to look
into the woods. Grown in close competition, the trees
were curved and irregular. They weren't giants, but the
brush beneath them was thick enough to make the
forest seem impenetrable.

The sand road on which I sat seemed to have nothing to do with New York and my problems. I'd taken
Gleason's side trip because I was afraid to end my day
empty-handed. It occurred to me now that the peace
of the forest was as much as I could hope to find, so I
lingered for a moment to enjoy it. I left the engine off
long enough for nearby birds to resume their calling.
When I turned the ignition key, my old car eliminated
the peace in a way that embarrassed and isolated me.

The rest of the directions were easy. I was to follow
the same sand road, taking the right fork whenever the
road divided. After a drive of three miles I would
come to Skiles's house, Gleason had told me. It would
be the first one I'd see.

It felt more like ten miles had passed before I found
the house. It was small and wider than it was deep, like
a house trailer with a gable roof. The roof was covered with wooden shingles, grayed from exposure. The
same shingles covered part of the outside walls. The
tar paper that had so impressed Gleason was tacked up
irregularly as part of what seemed to be an ongoing
renovation. The windows on either side of the front
door held one or two shingles in place of broken
panes. The door was the only item that looked re-

cently tended; it was painted an unexpected bright red. The door was approached by narrow stairs made from concrete blocks. The same type of blocks, in a series of pilings, held the house a foot or two off the ground.

There was nothing resembling a driveway, so I pulled up onto Skiles's front lawn. It was sand, too, and dried weeds, and it was decorated by an old refrigerator lying on its side and an even older water pump. The galvanized bucket that hung from the pump was still wet, I noted as I walked past. It was the only indication I could see, apart from the red front door, that the place was actually inhabited. I'd no sooner had that thought when a more convincing sign came from within the house itself: a single loud snap. I remembered Hinkle's warning about the Pineys and decided I'd heard the bolt on a gun. I remained next to the pump, wishing I'd turned the Volkswagen around before I'd parked it.

The man who opened the red door didn't have a gun. Allowing for Gleason's romance, he was about the right age, middle to late sixties. He had gray hair and a neatly trimmed gray beard. His face was brown and weathered, but the lines around his eyes looked like they'd come from a lifetime of laughing. The eyes were small and literally overshadowed by a large forehead and shaggy brows. His small size was accentuated by baggy olive drab trousers with rolled cuffs and a plaid woolen shirt that billowed around his waist.

"You lost, son?" the man asked me.

"Not if you're Jim Skiles," I said.

The wrinkles around his eyes deepened. "I don't know," he said. "You've got the look of a man who's lost somehow. I may be Jim Skiles, son, but you're still lost."

"Thanks," I said.

"I'll bet you've come seeking the wisdom of the ages." Skiles seemed to have quickly arrived at the same humorous disregard for me that Dr. Schiel had first shown.

I leaned on the rusty pump to demonstrate a calm I didn't feel. "Actually, I wanted some water for my radiator."

"That car of yours don't have a radiator."

"Then I guess I'll settle for the wisdom," I said. "Tim Gleason sent me."

Skiles laughed and extended an arm through his open doorway. "I thought that might be it," he said. "Come on in."

The room we entered was clean and sparsely furnished. It was a combination sitting and dining room. To my right as I entered was a small, drop-leaf table with two chairs. The table held a large, tin bread box. On the wall above it, there was a framed engraving, faded with age. It was a landscape identified in bold letters as Fairmount Park. An unpadded bench with a high slat back stood against the opposite wall. There were open doorways on both sides of the room. The smell of burning grease came from the doorway on my right.

"I'm sorry I interrupted your cooking," I said.

Skiles offered me a chair whose cane bottom had been replaced by a plywood square. "Wasn't cooking," he said. "Bought me a new cast-iron frying pan. I was just curing it. You ever cure a frying pan?"

"Not lately."

"Well, you gotta bake that grease on hard to do any good. Smells kind of strong now, but there won't be anything sticking to it when it's done. Just let me go check on it for a minute. I'll be right back.''

I sat obediently at the small table and waited. Somehow, Skiles and his ridiculous house had brought back the feeling of unreality I'd felt at the very beginning of my research. The events of the last two days had convinced me that a forty-year-old plane crash could have tangible connections to the world I lived in. Very tangible connections, in fact. Now I felt as though I were losing ground. I had landed myself in a place that seemed even more fanciful and meaningless than the Carteret story and less probable than my library books, despite the incidental detail of being real.

I found I was staring at the tin bread box. It was white and slightly rusted, with faded red flowers on the sides. The front was actually the lid, hinged at the bottom and fastened at the top with a metal catch, like a mailbox door. It occurred to me that the box's catch was the only thing in the room that could have produced the metallic snap I'd heard from the yard. To confirm my deduction, I raised the catch with my thumb and lowered the tin door. I still had the idea of a gun in the back of my mind, although it was now a smaller gun. Instead I found bread crumbs and a small book. The book surprised me. Gleason had described Skiles as illiterate.

I listened for a moment to the sounds coming from the kitchen. Skiles was humming to himself, softly. There was a sudden crackling, as though he had poured more grease into the hot pan. I took the book from the box and examined it. It was an old edition of Montaigne's essays, bound in blue leather. Inside the front cover, the name James Skiles was written in a regular hand with ink that had faded to purple. There was a Philadelphia address under the name, somewhere on Thirtieth Street. I replaced the book and closed the lid slowly, without allowing the catch to sound. My egotistical thought that the twists of a complicated plot were following wherever I led came back to me now like a warning.

Skiles came in, wiping his hands on a dirty towel. He tossed it through the doorway behind him before sitting down. "Tim Gleason sent you, did he? You remind me of Tim somehow."

"It's the nose," I said.

"I was thinking more of a look about the eyes. A searching kind of look. Questioning. The nose, you say? You kin to Tim?"

"Yes," I said, reaching thoughtlessly for a disguise.

"I'd consider that answer careful, if I was you. Tim's got a running tongue. Comes out here to listen to me and does most of the talking himself. I know quite a bit about his family."

"In that case, I met him for the first time this morning." I spoke indifferently, unable to shake the feeling that I'd stepped through a mirror and Skiles would shortly offer me tea.

Skiles didn't seem surprised or offended. "I don't believe you've told me your name yet, son."

"Owen Keane."

"Don't know any Keanes."

"Sorry."

"Don't matter. What was I talking about? Oh yeah, Tim's look. That boy is always asking questions. Even when he's talking about himself he's looking around, soaking things in. He writes for the newspaper, so I guess it's part of his job. You a newspaper man?''

"I'm trying to be. Right now I'm only working at it part time.''

"What do you do for a living?''

"I work in a law office.''

"You a lawyer?'' Skiles asked, his tiny eyes narrowing.

"No,'' I said.

"I can't abide lawyers. If a man's got principles, he thinks of justice. If he hasn't, he thinks of laws. In some languages lawyer and liar are the same word. Do you believe that?''

"I'm not a lawyer.''

"You didn't answer my question.''

"No, I don't believe that.''

Skiles gave me an elaborately sad look. "If it's not true, it should be,'' he said. "It's just too bad when life can't be like the truth.'' He brightened quickly. "You probably didn't come here for philosophy.'' He tilted his chair back on two legs and folded his hands across his small stomach. "Any stories you want to hear in particular? Tim really likes the ones about the pine robbers. They was highway men, only rougher and more cold blooded than any English robber. More like Wild West desperadoes. None of that 'stand and deliver.' They shot first and made their speeches later. There's a story my father used to tell about Joseph Mulliner, worst of a bad lot. He heard it from his father. Would you like to hear that one?''

"Gleason told me you like to know your audience before you tell a story.''

"I do, son, I do. But I get to know a person real fast. I know you already, son. You won't believe nine out of ten stories I tell you."

I played straight man. "Then why tell me any?" I asked.

"Because you'll believe the tenth story, and that's a damn sight more than most people today." Skiles laughed with enough enthusiasm to display gaps in his teeth. "Cut me any way you want, son, you get philosophy. How about it, will it be the Pine robbers?"

"What do you know about plane crashes in the Pines?"

"Carranza, you mean? The Lindbergh of Mexico? Oh, I know all about Carranza. Crashed near Hampton Furnace in 1928. Flying from New York to Mexico someplace. Got caught in a thunderstorm. There's still folks out that way claim to have heard his engine, but that's just moonshine. They didn't even find the wreckage till two days later, and then it was by accident."

"How about a wreck they didn't find for nine months?" I asked.

Skiles slowly let his chair down on four legs. "The house brand is sure wasted on you, son," he said. "William Carteret. I never told Tim Gleason no ghost stories. How did you come to hear of Carteret?"

I repeated my fiction on the difficulties of free-lance writing. My lack of enthusiasm for the second telling bounced back to me from the walls of the small room. As he listened, Skiles took a faded red bandanna from his hip pocket. He shook it out and began to fold it carefully on his knee.

"I was wrong before when I said you and Tim have the same questioning look," he began. "Tim's got it in his blood, if you know what I mean. Just instinctive. He asks his questions so fast, you know he can't be thinking them up between times." He considered his folded handkerchief briefly, shook it out, and started folding it again. "And it don't bother him to ask his questions. Don't cost him anything. Owen Keane don't seem to enjoy it, now that I study him. I wouldn't bother with the newspaper work if I was you."

"Were you living here when Carteret crashed?"

"Me? No. No, it wouldn't have taken them nine months to find the plane if I'd been here back then. You're sitting half a mile from the very spot. The last paved road you took, Five Thirty-nine, ain't more than a couple of miles from the spot as the crow flies. Carteret must have seen that road on his way down, must have looked like heaven to him, but he didn't make it. Fact is, if he'd cracked up in the deep woods they would have found him sooner. That's my opinion. The Pine people would have known he was there. But he was too close to the road for the Pineys and too far from the road for the people driving up from the ocean. Took a couple of city boys playing soldier to find what was left."

"Why do you call it a ghost story?" I asked.

"Because it is, is all. The only honest-to-God ghost story in this part of the woods. It's the only reason Carteret is even remembered around here. There was no monument built for him like there was for Carranza. Not even a stick, not from his family, I mean. I heard once that they owned half of Long Island. The only monument Carteret got was an old rock painted white. One of the state conservation people did it during the war. I don't know why. Probably couldn't find his way around the woods if he didn't have things painted.''

Skiles shook his bandanna out for the fourth time and smiled at me. "You're a patient man, Owen Keane, I'll give you that. You can wait a feller out. I like that about you.''

"Thanks.''

"Because of that, I'm going to tell you the tenth story I mentioned before. It's a ghost story, like I said, and it was first told by a simpleminded girl. She's dead now, been gone a good ten years, but she told it to me herself. I wish I had her here to tell you. Best proof of a story is the teller. This poor girl was too simple to lie. Just telling about that day would scare her to her hair roots.

"Her name was Blueberry Ann. That wasn't her real name, of course, but that's what everybody called her. Simple and fey, like a wild horse. I lived back in here a year before she ever come near my place. Years ago, people thought that all Pineys were simpleminded from inbreeding. Some probably still think so. Ain't true of the Pineys as a group, but it was true of Ann. Just a simple soul, the kind you can find in any part of the country.

"Ann made her living off the land, doing a little hunting, helping in the cranberry bogs, and picking wild blueberries. That's how she got her name, picking blueberries, so I guess she was pretty good at it. High bush blueberries are a big part of the understory, that's the growth beneath the trees, and they're really good eating.

"When Ann wasn't working or hunting, she'd just walk. That was her way of resting, just walking through the woods. I know this little part of the woods pretty well, but drop me twenty miles back, and I might lose my way. Any city folk would be lost for sure. Blueberry Ann never got lost. She'd just wander around, walking soft like an Indian, and by and by she'd wind her way back to her cabin. Some say God works in mysterious ways. Abundant compensation, I call it.''

"You and Wordsworth," I said.

"Who?"

"Never mind."

Skiles slapped his knee, knocking the folded bandanna to the floor. "I don't know what I've been thinking of," he said. "Man drives all the way out here, and I keep him sitting at a table. You'd probably like to see the place. Sure you would. Give you a real feel for the story."

TWENTY-TWO

SKILES LIMITED MY VIEW of his home by leading me out the way I'd come in. He paused for a moment on the steps to admire his front door.

"How do you like that?" he asked me. "I seen a red door on the cover of a ladies' magazine last time I was up to Bargersville. Just had to have one."

I followed him across the barren lot. "You don't have electricity here, do you?"

"Nope. Never had any to this house."

I kicked the frayed electrical cord that snaked from the back of the refrigerator. "Then where did you plug this in?" I asked.

Skiles was examining the sky. "That's a good question. Look up at those clouds, will you. They look thick enough to walk on and close enough to touch. You cold, son?"

"I'm fine."

"Feels chilly to me. Feels like we're going to have an early winter."

We walked toward Five Thirty-nine on the sand road. Skiles was quiet for the moment, so I took a break myself. The clouds I'd noted at the beach did seem more densely packed now, and lower. The pines on either side of the road were no more than thirty feet tall, but the gray sky seemed to be resting on top of them. It occurred to me that humoring Skiles was a waste of time I didn't have, but I was intrigued by the idea that William Carteret had become a local legend.

Perhaps his unquiet spirit was trying to pass on the clue I needed. My curiosity made me unwary.

"Hear that bird, son?" Skiles asked me. "Listen."

"I hear it," I said. Its call was a pair of trills, low followed by high.

"It's the call of the Eastern Bluebird. Here we go, son, off to your right here." Skiles indicated a narrow path. "It's back in here a ways. Go ahead. Don't worry, I won't get you in too deep. I don't think we'll be bothered by snakes this time of year, but I'd watch those sticker bushes. You sure didn't dress for this expedition. I'll walk behind you, so you can hear me better."

The path was covered with pine needles. In leather oxfords I walked silently enough to belittle Blueberry Ann's Indian abilities. The pine trees helped to cover the little noise we made. Their tops swayed in the stiffening breeze, with a sound like rushing water. The rustling of the dry underbrush contributed during exceptionally strong gusts. The trees were thick on either side of the path, and they deformed each other in their competition for the light. We passed a dead, bare trunk, bleached white but held upright by its neighbors, and a living tree that had grown horizontally, searching for its own bit of sun. Skiles read my thoughts. "Like people in a city," he said. Beneath the pines I saw an occasional hollow tree. Below them, most of the green that was left belonged to the ferns.

"You know that bird don't you son?" Skiles spoke conversationally, but I could hear him clearly over the sounds of the forest.

"Whippoorwill," I said.

"Good for you. You're a regular scout. Little early in the evening for that gentleman to be singing. Must be the overcast fooling him. This is just the way Ann used to wander, except that she wasn't so mindful of the path. Take the left fork here, son. This'll give you an idea of what it was like that day. Carteret crashed about this time of year, as I recall.''

"October tenth," I said. "Today's the seventh."

"This'll be the fortieth anniversary," Skiles said. "Hard to believe. Mind if I ask you a question, son?"

"Go ahead."

"Why did you lie to me back at the house? About being Tim's kin, I mean."

"I don't know," I said. The question embarrassed me, as it was intended to do. Thinking back, it seemed as though I'd lied to everyone I'd met in connection with the Carteret business, one way or another.

"Maybe it was because you are a lawyer, after all. You know, lawyer and liar are the same word in some languages."

"I told you before I wasn't a lawyer."

"Your word's no good to me, son. That's the Pine Siskin you're hearing now. Real pretty bird."

"Five minutes ago it was the Eastern Bluebird."

Skile's laugh had a dry cackle at the end. "Yep, son, you're right. That's just a little joke I play on city folks. I had Tim Gleason believing that was everything but a great horned owl. You may be a liar, but you have a good ear."

Skiles had succeeded in making me angry. I stopped and turned on him. "I thought I had a good ear myself," I said, "but I'm having a little trouble with the way you talk, Mr. Skiles."

"Sorry about that, son. Good grammar ain't something we put much stock in here. Don't buy you anything."

"Your grammar isn't as bad as it is inconsistent. That's not what I mean exactly. There was a time when I could tell where a man was from just by listening to him talk."

"Is that right?"

"It was taught to me by George Bernard Shaw," I said, carried away by my embarrassment and anger. "Believe it or not, I would have placed you in Philadelphia. On Thirtieth Street. Somewhere near Fairmount Park, I think."

Skiles's gap-toothed smile disappeared. For a second, he looked frightened. "Who sent you?" he demanded.

"Tim Gleason sent me. I found your book in your damn bread box. That's all I know about you."

Skiles chewed on my explanation. "I hope you're not laughing at me," he said.

"I'm not," I replied, cooling with every word. "I'm just trying to explain why I lied to you. I guess I wanted to be somebody else. I may be tired of who I am."

We watched each other in silence for longer than I liked. "I thought you were going to tell me a ghost story," I finally said.

"We'll stay on this path a ways," Skiles said, "go on ahead." I did as Skiles asked. I thought I had talked my way out of the story, but after a long silence he began.

"The funny thing about this story is that it took place in broad daylight. Better day than today, in fact. Not a cloud in the sky. Most times a ghost story needs a moonless night or somesuch for atmosphere. Of course, to some folks the pine forest at noon is as lonesome a place as any cemetery at midnight, so maybe it's not so funny after all.

"Blueberry Ann was out wandering that day when she heard a crashing sound in the brush. I told you Ann was a hunter. She'd heard a lot of game in the woods, and this sound was nothing like any of that. Not even like a buck scared up by some fool hunter from Mount Holly. Ann thought right away it was a man. She stood stock-still, the kind of still that'll bring a deer up close if the wind is right. The crashing noise got closer. Pretty soon, Ann heard another noise. It was a kind of sobbing, and, with it, she saw some movement through the trees.

"A year it took little Annie to come up and shake hands with me, but she stood her ground that day and waited. The man she saw was a stranger. He was wearing a leather jacket, and he had a green scarf around his neck. Bright green, kelly green, they call it. His face was bone white, except where it was smeared with blood. His hands were covered with blood, too."

I stopped walking. Skiles stepped up close to me on the narrow path. "The stranger was stumbling and kicking and swinging his way through the forest, like he wanted to hurt it somehow. All the time, he was drawing his breath in sobs. He passed within twenty yards of Ann and never saw her. His eyes were wide open, but he didn't see a thing. Not in this world anyway.

"When the thing had passed her, Ann turned and ran. Ran as fast as she could through everything but the pine trees themselves. I told you before that Ann never got lost in these woods. That isn't exactly true. Fact is, she got lost the day she saw that thing. Or maybe it was just her way of hiding. Wandered all night without recognizing a tree, she told me. But listening all night, too. Listening for a crashing and a sobbing noise coming up from behind her.''

Standing a foot from Skiles, I could see his small, red-veined eyes beneath the protruding brow. Something in their set of intensity made me appreciate Ann's terror more than the words of the story.

''Ann stayed away from this part of the forest for a time,'' Skiles said. ''But she worked the cranberry harvest up to Bargersville later that year, and she told some of the folks about seeing the thing in the woods. They laughed at her. Simpleminded Blueberry Ann. She didn't tell her story after that. Not for a while.

''The next year, those two soldiers came across the wreck of the plane. It had what was left of two bodies in it. One of them was a woman. The other was a man wearing a leather jacket. Around his neck, he had a green scarf. His skull was crushed. William Carteret.

''One or two of them cranberry harvesters remembered Ann's story when they heard about the wreck. I talked to one of them years later, a feller named Bill Herrode. He swore to me that Ann had described that dead pilot, and Herrode was a sober kind of man. It made me want to hear about it from the horse's mouth. I bided my time with Ann. I caught that story of hers like catching a bird under a box, by sitting patient and waiting. She told it to me one day during a walk through these woods. I've been looking over my shoulder for William Carteret ever since.

''You may think that's funny, but Blueberry Ann wasn't the last person to see Carteret's ghost. I've heard tell of one or two others, and more than that claim to have heard a rustling noise in this part of the forest, and a sobbing along with it.''

Skiles had thrown the story down before me like a
challenge to an unbelieving world. He stood waiting
for me to pick it up, with his bearded chin extended.
Offending him seemed stupid and pointless to me now,
but I couldn't find a conciliatory word.

"Should we be heading back?" I asked.

"We can if you want, Mr. Keane, but we're almost
to the spot. Come a long way not to see it."

"How far?"

"Another five minutes, maybe. Afraid we're going
to have to break our own trail now. Follow me."

Skiles set off at a brisk pace through the dry underbrush, pausing only to hold a pine branch or a thorny
bush back so I could pass. He did this service without
looking at me and without acknowledging my thanks.
Our pace made the forest seem warm, despite the
wind.

In a tiny clearing carpeted with small ferns, Skiles
stopped and scratched his chin. "That rock should be
right here," he said. "I might have left the trail too
soon, but I don't believe so. No sir, it should be close
by. I'm going to poke around to the left here a little.
You do the same on the right. We're looking for a
rounded rock about knee high. Just holler if you find
it. And don't stray far from this clearing, hear me? I
don't fancy spending the night looking for you."

He turned without waiting for a reply, and stepped
into the trees on the left. He studied the ground as he
went, parting the underbrush in his careful way. I
watched for a moment as he moved along the rim of
the open space. Then I left the clearing myself.

I found the rock right away. It was awash in an
overflow of ferns from the clearing, five paces from
the edge. It was no longer white, but a trace of the old

paint remained in its cracks and depressions, making it look like the globe of a frozen moon. It seemed at least that far removed from the Long Island estate with the tall green fence. The very spot, as Skiles had called it. The spot where Lynn Baxter and somebody named Carteret had died. I still had no real idea who or why.

I'd come a long way myself during my search, a long way from my cozy library and the mindless rut I'd dug for myself. Now I stood where the "glist'ring" *Phaeton* had come to rest when its momentum would carry it no farther. I felt I'd also come as far as the emotional momentum of the last few days would carry me. I'd come to earth in precisely the same spot as the *Phaeton* had, as though in obedience to some unbending physical law, and in the same desperate shape, with no answers to my questions and no second chance.

I stepped back into the clearing. "I found it," I said. Skiles didn't answer. I turned in a full circle, looking for a sign of his plaid shirt in the swaying movement of the trees. "Skiles," I called out, "I've found your damn rock." This time I heard the dry cackle of Skiles laughing at me from somewhere in the forest.

TWENTY-THREE

I YELLED AT THE FOREST for a few minutes. I like to think it was only a few minutes anyway. I was really yelling at myself. Once again, I had treated another person's pretense carelessly. With Skiles, I wasn't going to talk my way out of it. I'd tried invective and threats during my yelling phase, and now I briefly considered reason. I had an idea that Skiles was somewhere nearby, hanging by his feet from a tree and enjoying my situation. But the idea of apologizing to the pine trees at large made me despair before I began. Instead, I went back to Carteret's frozen moon and sat down.

At that moment, I didn't think of the forest as the real threat. I was more afraid of Skiles. I mentally retraced our walk from his house, and decided that it had been straightforward enough. The only questionable part was the five-minute struggle from the path to the clearing where I now sat. I wasn't anxious to arrive at Skiles's house, not if his only motive for deserting me was to get a head start, but I couldn't think of an alternative.

I left the clearing at the point where Skiles and I had entered it. I had convinced myself that I could follow the trail we had ''broken'' through the bush, but I was surprised to find how little there was to follow. Skiles had had a reason for parting the branches so carefully for me that had nothing to do with protecting my clothes. There was no possibility of tracks in the pine needle carpet beneath the dry underbrush. I tried to recognize a familiar tree, and found that they all looked familiar. I blamed myself for not studying the forest after we left the path. I had been too busy thinking of the ghost of William Carteret. That recollection made me look back over my shoulders, as I had in Dr. Schiel's silent hallway. The reflex didn't seem as silly now.

I'd struggled on for five minutes when I had the thought that Skiles might have led me from the path in a long arc, to keep me from walking straight back. Five minutes later, it occurred to me that he could have broken a false trail after he'd left me in the clearing, intending to start me toward the deep woods. Ten minutes after that, I finally admitted to myself that I was lost.

A growing inclination to panic worked like a drug on my tired brain. I thought of things that had no relation to finding my way out of the forest. I thought of Carolyn Vernia's bizarre office decoration, the threatening girder, somehow juxtaposing it with the praying hands on Mildred Tucker's wall. My mind played meaningless games with the names of the people I'd stumbled across, until the details of the case seemed like the makings of a nursery rhyme. Vernia, Carolyn to Carteret, William to Warden. Gus to Gregson, Peter to Parnell, Lois to Lynn Baxter to Bill Herrode to Harry Greb to Gleason, Tim to Tucker, Mildred to Marilyn Tucci. Only to Marilyn for a moment, and then back to Carolyn Vernia, waiting in her cavernous office for me to pass beneath the girder. She had described my problem politely enough: a mind that tends to wander dangerously without occupation. My mind had occupation enough now and it had almost wandered off the map. I folded my own hands from old habit and tried to gather myself.

I finally forced my attention outside of my head by calculating the remaining daylight. I figured that there was less than an hour left. I then tried to determine my nearest landmark. Skiles's house should have been to the northwest, but it was too small a target to hope to hit. The sand road I had followed from Five Thirty-nine was better, but I had no idea how far past his house it extended. If I strayed too far to the west, I might walk around it in the dark. So far, my reasoning seemed sound, if depressing. The methodical effort had even calmed me somewhat. My only choice was Highway Five Thirty-nine itself. It was to the east, I decided, no more than three to five miles away.

"So far so good," I said aloud. The words seemed to echo inside me like a child's taunt. Alone in a forest, except for a crazy hermit. No one who would miss me even knew what state I was in. So far so good. I had fallen into a trap, I thought. My own.

The nursery rhyme voice began again in my head. "Figure out which way is east," I said in my own voice. The sky was no help. The only thing the homogeneous gray above the trees told me was to hurry. I examined the pine trees for moss, but their flaky bark seemed immune. Then I remembered something more valuable: the branches on the south side of a tree are the longest. I checked several trees before making my best guess. The difference was dubious in the crowded forest where no limb seemed to grow straight, but I convinced myself that it was discernible.

I struck out to the east as quickly as the dry tangle beneath the trees would allow, knowing that darkness would soon make the southern branches useless to me. The bushes and even the strange vines that dropped in groups of four or five from the trees were covered with thorns. I was careless of myself and my clothes in an effort to walk as straight a line as possible. I used the most distant tree I could distinguish as an intermediate goal. It was never more than twenty yards away. I only stopped long enough to check my heading with the branches overhead when a particularly dense thicket forced a detour. Each time I stopped, the tops of the trees became harder to see.

The sound of the trees was rising with the wind. I heard what I thought was a woodpecker, some distance away. Skiles's universal bird was no longer calling. Maybe it had never called, I thought. Maybe Skiles was a ventriloquist on top of everything else. His quiet voice had carried easily enough. I tried my own voice against the forest. "God damn it," I said aloud. My words were swept away by the rushing wind and hidden in the rustling of the brush. I thought of Blueberry Ann, straining her ears to hear a sobbing in the same wind. It strengthened my resolve not to relive her night in the forest.

The effort required to walk my straight line wasn't enough to keep my mind from wandering again. I thought of Marilyn, riding home to Brooklyn in a swaying subway car, alone in a sullen, unspeaking crowd. Marilyn was always alone, I reflected, even in a crowd. Cut off and isolated like her fellow subway riders by the sad idea that the universe extended no farther than they could see. I didn't accept that con-vention myself, but at that moment—in a darkening forest complete with its own ghost and madman—my expanded universe was not a consolation. To distract my imagination, I reran my presentation for Carolyn Vernia, looking for coincidence that could be replaced by motive. The key to any successful investigation, I told myself, was explaining away coincidence and chance. That, and not dying of exposure in a pine forest. One coincidence that I didn't try to dismiss was the odd fact that the Carteret business had come my way in the first place. The possibility that it hadn't been by chance, that it was the result of some directed action, was more frightening to me than the coming night.

I was taking a final bearing in the fading light, when I heard a branch snap somewhere behind me. I wasted a full minute waiting for another sound. None came. It might have been William Carteret, coming to tell me the secret of his death, but I was no longer anxious for the answer. There was a more likely explanation in any case. Skiles had grown tired of waiting for me. Now he was following me. The thought did wonders for my flagging pace.

It was fully dark when I saw the headlights through the trees. I was twenty minutes past my last direction check by then. I could see almost as far as the branches I was parting with outstretched arms. I was too tired to lift my feet clear of the underbrush, and I fell twice during the last ten yards. My feelings of relief and gratitude were genuine, but they only carried me as far as the edge of the forest. By the time I reached the pavement, I'd begun to calculate the odds of another car passing before dawn.

I also thought of Skiles. I crossed the road to put two lanes of worn civilization between us. It turned out to be another of my futile gestures. Skiles was standing on the opposite side of the road, waiting for me.

"Way you started, son, you might have thought I was William Carteret himself," Skiles said.

The darkness and the distance I kept made him difficult to see, in spite of his plaid work shirt, but as far as I could tell, Skiles was as chipper and friendly as when we'd first met. He would have frightened me less if he'd been as angry as I was.

It took me a moment to find my voice. "Get the hell away from me."

Skiles laughed at my attempt to intimidate him. "I told you back at the house that I knew you, son. You wouldn't hit a dog."

"I know a lawyer in New York who could argue that with you."

"Oh, every man has his breaking point. I know that. But I was watching you the whole time. You were nowhere near over your head. You even had me fooled a bit when you decided to make for the road. Yep, you did real well."

"I'm a regular scout, remember?"

"Yep."

As far as I could tell, Skiles was unarmed, but there was something in his happy voice that worried me more than the gun I'd imagined earlier. He was the closest thing to a real ghost I would find in the Pines, and I didn't want his company.

"Come on back to the house now," Skiles said.

"No thanks. Buy yourself some white mice."

"I'm serious, son. I've been thinking it over. I want to tell you why I left my life in Philadelphia and how I came to be in the woods."

Skiles the storyteller was offering to tell me the only tale that was really his. Mad as I was, I was curious, but I had no intention of following him back into his realm.

"I'll be back in the daylight for my car," I said. "You can tell me your story then."

For the first time, I had trouble hearing his voice. "I'm not crazy," he said.

Skiles's quiet statement had a familiar ring to it. Maybe it was because it was the motto of our century. Or maybe I heard an echo of my own protests to Marilyn and the world. The echo might have softened me in the daylight or on a crowded street. But in the dark forest I was too isolated.

I heard the sound of a car coming from behind me. I turned in time to see its headlights signaling through the trees that lined a bend in the road.

Skiles came toward me out of the darkness. "Come back to the house, Mr. Keane. I need you to listen to this. Look out, now. You'll get yourself run over."

I'd stepped out into the road to wave the car down. Fortunately, it was beyond setting any records, except for longevity. It was a station wagon, and it pulled over ten yards past me. Skiles grabbed at my coat as I ran to the car. A man and a woman shared the front seat. I silently hoped that they would be impressed by my jacket and tie or at least that they wouldn't notice the dirt and the other damage.

I asked for a ride to a phone.

"Hop in," the woman said.

Skiles hadn't given up. "How about your car?" he asked. "You are coming back?" I could still hear him as the wagon pulled away. "I'll look after the car," he called. "You come on back to see me."

TWENTY-FOUR

"YOU HAVE AN ACCIDENT or something?" the man at the wheel asked me. There was a scrambling noise behind me as he spoke. Something crawled past me in the dark and up into the front seat. It smelled like a dog.

"My car broke down back in the woods," I said. "I had to walk out."

"Back in the woods, you say?" The woman turned to look at me. She seemed to be about retirement age, but her eyes were wide and innocent. "Whatever were you doing back in there?" she asked.

My reply confirmed Skiles's worst opinion of me. "Collecting samples," I said. "I'm a botanist from the University of Pennsylvania. We think we've discovered a new type of fern in the Pines. It's pretty exciting."

Our driver grunted at that, but the woman sounded impressed. "No kidding," she said.

"Who was that other guy?" the man asked.

"Local guide."

"No kidding."

"No kidding," I said.

Their name was Thompson and they lived near Allentown. I recognized the name of the town, associating it with a quiet crossroads ten miles or so east of Trenton, and it sounded like a step in the right direction. Mr. Thompson agreed to take me that far. The drive lasted about an hour, which gave Mrs. Thompson and me time for a long talk. Their two children were grown and gone. One was a pharmacist in Cherry Hill. The other did something with computers in Harrisburg. During the drive, I developed a wife and two kids of my own. We lived in a renovated townhouse near Fairmount Park. Inflation was killing us. My oldest girl would need braces in a year or two.

My imaginary family drove off in the old station wagon with the Thompsons, leaving me on a dimly lit Allentown street corner. I felt as though I'd gotten the worst part of the deal.

Allentown was a good place to be lonely. It wasn't quite seven o'clock, but the local sidewalk department was already rolling them up. I'd worked out a plan during the drive. I'd hitchhike to Trenton and catch a train to New York City. Unfortunately, I'd used up all my luck landing my ride with the Thompsons. It took me an hour to reach Hamilton, one of Trenton's fat suburbs. From there, I took an expensive cab ride into the crumbling heart of the old city.

Trenton was my hometown, but there was no home for me there anymore. No family and no old friends who would smile if I showed up on their doorstep. No roots, I thought, as my cab carried me past blocks of quiet row homes. That sad reflection made me wonder how much better off I was in Trenton than I'd been in Skiles's forest. How well off I was anywhere, in fact.

The Trenton train station was a modern glass and metal shell built atop platforms and tracks that hadn't changed in my lifetime. In a men's room that needed cleaning, I tried to repair the outward signs of my march through the forest. The scratches on my face and a wood tick I found in my hair contradicted the dreamlike quality that episode had already taken on. Another bit of evidence I still carried was my barely controlled paranoia. In the dirty, overheated lavatory, I still had the feeling of being lost. To escape it, I left the station that I didn't recognize and descended to the familiar platform.

The next train to New York wouldn't leave for an hour, and the platform was almost deserted. The only person I could see was a young man dressed in dirty work clothes and a baseball cap. He was lying on one of the old wooden benches that I'd played on as a child. As I walked past him, he opened his eyes.

"You just missed the eight o'clock," he said.

"Yes," I said as I moved on. My time alone in the woods hadn't improved my casual social behavior. Besides which, he smelled like Skiles.

I began to pace up and down the long platform. I was tired, but I still felt like moving, as though I'd lose some important momentum if I sat down, as though walking back and forth across the dirty concrete was carrying me toward a goal. I told myself that it was just Trenton, triggering the same survival instinct that had carried me out of the forest. That thought started a short chain of thoughts, a calmer version of the nursery rhyme I'd barely controlled in the forest. At first I felt proud of my escape from the forest and of my small adventure. I remembered, then, the ghost of William Carteret and the story I'd tried not to consider too closely while I was within the range of Skiles's imagination. Thinking of it reminded me that I'd heard another ghost story recently, or something like one. It wasn't hard to place, even in my tired mind. Miller, the bank guard, had told it to me the night before.

Then I understood the Carteret mystery. I knew the murderer, the victim, and the crime. My half-steps and turnings of the last few days became a logical sequence, a straight line that led from Harry's office to this empty platform easily and inevitably.

"Don't fall off there." The man with the baseball cap was now sitting up on his bench. My epiphany had come at the far end of the platform. I found myself a foot from the edge, staring at the garbage and loose stone by the side of the roadbed.

"You okay?" the man asked.

"Great," I said as I trotted past him. I took the stairs up into the station two at a time. I found a phone booth and called Harry's home number. Mary, his wife and my once-upon-a-time love, answered.

"Hello again," I said.

"Owen?"

"Yes," I said, secretly pleased that she'd recognized my voice.

"Owen, you've had us all worried."

"'All'? You're starting to sound like Harry."

"Both of us, I mean. Don't pare it down any further. Harry is worried, too."

"He enjoys it," I said.

"Are you home now?"

"How's the baby?" I asked.

"She's fine," Mary said.

"It's good to hear your voice, Mary."

"Owen." She used my name to signal a stop in the small talk.

"I'm in Trenton," I said. "I was trying to lead up to it gracefully. I haven't enough change to explain how I got here. You'll have to wait for Harry's version. It won't be sympathetic."

"Harry's not here. He's still in town. I have a number where he can be reached. Some business came to a head today."

"I'm the business, Mary."

She wasn't surprised to hear it. "I know what you're thinking," Mary said, "but Harry's on your side. He's called our apartment every hour."

"He's a prince, I know."

Mary adopted a tone of reproof. "Harry's been good to you."

"To us," I said, "but I don't care to discuss his good points while I'm trying to sweet-talk his wife."

"Save the charm, Owen. One accidental phone call a year doesn't entitle you."

"There's more than that, Mary."

"If you get sentimental, I'll know you've been drinking."

"I'll be all business then. Tell Harry I need to talk with him tomorrow morning at the office. First thing. I've cracked the Carteret case. I forgot to tell you, I grew up to be a famous detective."

"You've never grown up," Mary said.

I noted with gratitude that Mary made the statement without sadness. In fact, she almost sounded pleased. I loved her all over again then. "Will you tell him?" I asked.

"I can give you the number..."

"No. My train's leaving any minute. I want to get to the city before they lock the back door."

"I'll tell him," she said.

"Sorry to keep your husband out so late."

"Don't worry about it. At least tonight I know what he's up to."

"Mary. You don't have to worry about Harry. He's a prince, remember?"

"I don't care to discuss my husband's good points with a man who's supposed to be sweet-talking me. It's good to hear your voice, too, Owen. Are you going to be okay?"

"Absolutely."

"Owen."

"Yes, I'll be fine."

I'd already seen a day's worth of New Jersey, and my tour wasn't finished. My return to New York would take me over familiar ground, the old railroad line that ran through the heart of the state. The train that finally arrived at the Trenton platform was a colorless commuter, owned and operated by New Jersey Transit. I found a seat in one of their new plastic coaches that looked like the inside of a square airliner. The cosmetic improvements stopped at the tinted windows. The stations I watched come and go were depressing representatives of their cities. New Brunswick, Metuchen, Rahway, Elizabeth. Depressing because they were old and dirty and deserted and because their time had passed. Talking with Mary had made me sentimental without a drink. Or nostalgic. Or maybe I had spent too much time in the forties with the Carterets. I closed my eyes and pretended to sleep until Penn Station.

TWENTY-FIVE

I DIDN'T GO to my apartment. I stayed on the subway past my stop, got off at the next station, and walked to Marilyn's building. I'd been heading for it when I left the clearing of the ferns. All Skiles's woodlore hadn't told him that. I hadn't known it myself. I was afraid to go to my own place. Afraid that I'd fall asleep and wouldn't hear them when they came through the door. Afraid that they'd be in my apartment already. Afraid that I carried them with me. The lights were on in Marilyn's apartment, which gave me the heart to go on. She never made love with the lights on. I took advantage of a young couple's noisy departure and slipped through the security door without calling ahead. Another Keane victory.

I walked up the narrow, twisting stairs to her apartment, feeling the weight in my legs and thinking it was a gift, an anchor. I could hear the pounding beat of her stereo from the top of the hall. I knocked on her door loudly and stood back in the weak hall light so she could study me through her milky peephole.

"Owen, is that you?"

"It's the cat. I've brought you a dead mouse."

There was an indecisive silence in the room beyond the door. It was followed by another small triumph, the rattle of her security chain. Removing the chain turned out to be a gesture on her part, and not of goodwill. Marilyn opened the door to the width of her shoulders and moved forward a half step to block the opening. She was wearing a bathrobe and her hair was combed back from her face and tightly pinned. Her robe and her hair contradicted the evidence of the liquor on her breath and confirmed my earlier hope. She was alone.

"Did you have to fight for that mouse?" she asked.

"What?"

"Your face is scratched."

"Yes," I said. "I'm wounded. There's a danger of infection." My voice was much happier than I was. There was more energy to it, almost a laughing quality. It wasn't a good sign.

"Go take a bath," Marilyn said.

"Offer me a drink. I want to celebrate."

"I haven't got anything to drink."

"I'll take a glass of that mouthwash you're using."

"Go away, Keane."

"Would you ask me to leave if you thought I wouldn't come back?"

"It's never occurred to me. And anyway I'm not asking you. I'm telling you." She was telling me without conviction, however, so I held my ground. "What are you celebrating?" she finally asked.

"I've been born again," I said. "I need baptizing. Scotch is good."

"Tequila," she countered. "Take it or leave it." She let the door swing open as she turned away from me. "There's a glass in the kitchen and salt if you want it. I don't have any lime left." She walked to the stereo and turned it down. "After you're baptized, you can tell me what the hell you're talking about."

I walked into the kitchen, enjoying the novelty of the situation. For once, someone was waiting for me to reveal something. As a questioner, I'd always felt myself at a disadvantage. A buyer in a seller's market. I indulged myself now, selecting a drinking glass carefully and pouring the tequila like a chemist.

When I returned to the living room, Marilyn was sitting on the arm of her sofa, arranging and rearranging the tattered ends of her robe. She addressed me before she looked up. "I take it your doctor friend didn't beat you to death with a tongue depressor."

"I'll show you the splinters later," I said.

She watched me sip my drink for a moment. "You're off again, aren't you," she said.

The calm statement made me revert to questioner. "What do you mean?" I asked.

"You're off on your tangent," Marilyn said. With a shrug of concession she added, "Your search."

"I've solved a mystery," I said. "I haven't done that in a long time. I worked it out tonight, an hour or two ago. It's turned the calendar back for me, Marilyn. It's given me new hope."

My cheerful delivery was getting Marilyn down. "Through wisdom you cannot know God, Keane," she said.

"I've never had to worry about wisdom. What do you say, do you want to be born again?"

"Your hands are shaking. What's the matter?"

I looked down to confirm her observation. The hand that held the glass was twitching enough to make the liquor dance. "The answer cost me a little, I guess. Purification process or something. I've been wandering in the wilderness. Eating grasshoppers."

"You sure you weren't smoking them?" Marilyn asked with something like her old bravado. To my surprise, she moved from the arm of the sofa to the cushion beside me. Her expression hadn't softened, but she had, somehow. "What am I going to do with you?" she asked.

"Take me in tonight. I don't want to be alone."

"You're not a very confident convert."

"There are a lot of enemies of belief out there."

"I'm one of them."

"You don't believe, Marilyn, but you'd like to. I'm safe with you."

"You're never going to find out, Keane."

How many times had I heard that taunt? Often, it seemed. But it had never been expressed so softly before. "Humor me for a while," I said.

"For a while."

My hands might have been shaking, but my racing mind was slowing down. I finished the last of my tequila. Marilyn sat patiently, as though I'd been telling her a story and I was only halfway through. My story couldn't have a conventional ending. It would always be like the report I'd given Carolyn Vernia, blank pages on which you scrawled your best guess.

The bleak prospect seemed unimportant at the moment. "You are beautiful, Marilyn," I said. "And kind. And good. You're entitled to more than you think."

She reached out and touched my lips for a moment to silence me. "I'm past that kind of stuff, okay?"

"I'm not."

"I know," she said. "That's part of your problem. You're still fighting fights that ended a long time ago."

"I don't fight," I said. "I wouldn't hit a dog."

"I mean, you still worry about things that people have stopped worrying about. Questions that have been answered."

"How answered?" I asked.

"With a knock on the head."

I didn't have anything to say to that, so I listened to the cryptic mantra coming from the stereo. After a moment, Marilyn put her arms around me. It would have been a good time to cry, but I was years past the right tears. I held her instead, until my eyes became heavy with sleep.

"I like old questions," I heard myself say. "The new ones scare me."

"I know," Marilyn said.

TWENTY-SIX

THE FRONT-DESK receptionist at Ohlman, Ohlman, and Pulsifer looked at me as though I were a stranger. She always did, but on that morning I returned the compliment. I'd approached the Johnson Tyre Building several times before I'd actually gone in. Something about it hadn't seemed right. My hesitation had made me late, but that didn't worry me. I moved slowly through the familiar forest of desks, acoustical dividers, and filing cabinets toward Harry's office door. Ms. Kiefner's desk was standing at ease. I couldn't imagine her missing the show, unless Harry had planned it that way. She'd left a red rose in a tall crystal vase on the corner of her desk. I took the flower as I passed, the last desperate act of a desperate man. I stopped short of the threshold of Harry's office.

There was an angry discussion going on beyond the door. Two men were speaking at once. One of them was Harry. A woman's voice broke in and silenced them both. I recognized Carolyn Vernia's flat delivery. I opened the door a slow inch and listened.

"If you two want to argue, go out in the hall. You're giving me a headache. It's bad enough to be made to wait like this without having to listen to two lawyers fencing. I'm past being interested in a forensic exercise on discretion, Mr. Ohlman. Your firm's reputation is of no use to me when you can't even account for your staff."

"I don't have to account for his movements, Miss Vernia, to be accountable for his actions," Harry said.

"Brilliant. If I didn't already know you're a lawyer, that clever thrust would have told me."

I'd heard enough. I had no problem with eavesdropping, but I couldn't let Harry face her sarcasm alone.

I opened the door wide enough to admit my head. "Hello, the office," I said.

"Come on in, Owen." Harry sounded uncomfortable. "We've been waiting."

"I couldn't find the right building," I said.

Harry was seated at his desk, which surprised me. I somehow expected him to have deferred to his guest of honor. The two visitors were seated symmetrically in front of him with their backs to me. Carolyn Vernia's head barely showed above the back of her chair. The other head was a grizzled gray that turned profile toward me as I approached. It was a good profile, with a high-arched patrician nose. He hadn't turned his head to see me, I realized. He was waiting to see his companion's reaction.

"Full house," I said.

Harry rose to retrieve a straight-backed antique chair that sat between two bookcases. He placed it on his side of the desk.

Carolyn Vernia spoke as I passed her. "Have we surprised you, Mr. Keane?"

"Not really." I handed her the rose. "I picked that myself."

Harry was still standing with his hands on the back of my chair. "You didn't specify a private talk, Owen."

"I didn't have the heart, Harry."

I was a step or two from the chair before he noticed the marks on my face. "What happened to you? You look like you lost a fight."

I wanted to come back with a witty remark, but my entrance had taken something out of me. "Tough day at the library," was all I could manage.

"You weren't at the library. I looked there myself."

I started to ask him if he'd met Marilyn, but I changed my mind. I couldn't handle another conspiracy at the moment. "You're not going to guess where I've been, Harry," I said. "But if you sit down, I'll tell you."

"Mr. Ohlman informs us that you've arrived at a final solution," Vernia said. "It had better be an improvement on the one you told me."

"It's more of a variation," I said.

"I'd like to hear it now, if you don't mind."

"You have to eat your vegetables before you get the dessert, Miss Vernia." Harry flinched visibly at that. "You might as well relax, because we've got a lot of ground to cover first. For openers, I haven't met your friend."

"It can't be that difficult a deduction," the gray-haired profile said.

"Lawrence Bonsett, then."

"How do you do?"

"Fine."

"Really?" he asked. "You look done in."

"So I've heard. I'll hold up for another hour or so, I think."

Harry cleared his throat loudly to remind me that he still paid the rent on the office. "Sit down, Owen," he said.

I turned the chair around so the rigid back was facing our guests and straddled it with my arms folded across the top. Harry didn't like that, but I did. I felt less like I'd been called to the principal's office.

"Miss Vernia has told us about your talk," Harry said. "And about your theory."

"It was very inventive," Bonsett said. "It took me the better part of a morning to disprove it. Let me see, your solution rested on William Carteret sabotaging the plane and entering the army in Robert's place. Quite an idea. Unfortunatey, Robert was fingerprinted as part of a preinduction physical that took place in September, a month before the crash. We obtained a copy of his army records years ago when the original trust was set up. We never thought of checking the fingerprints, of course. To make a long story short, Mr. Carteret's prints matched those in the records."

"I hope you remembered to wipe the ink off his fingers," I said.

Harry cleared his throat again. "We three met last night so I could be brought up to date on the situation, including Mr. Carteret's present condition. I've assured Miss Vernia that our firm will not be guilty of any indiscretion on the subject and that your inquiries have always been directed solely to satisfying Mr. Carteret's commission. That brings us to the moment, I think."

It also tied Harry and Bonsett for speeches. Carolyn Vernia had begun tapping the arm of her chair halfway through the opening remarks. I couldn't figure out why she was so uncomfortable, unless it was the unfamiliar ground. Bonsett, in contrast, appeared to be falling asleep.

I smiled at them. "I'll try to be brief," I said.

"Try to be coherent, Mr. Keane," Vernia said.

Her sharp tone roused Bonsett. He sat up straight and made an effort at being pleasant. "You were going to tell us what you were up to yesterday," he said.

I'd been stalling up to that point. Jim Skiles would have appreciated my hesitation. Telling any story well requires judgment and timing. I had a long story ahead of me and an audience that wouldn't love me when it was over. It was also my story, my work, and my whole act. When the telling was over, a lot of things would be over. So I made a bid for a few more minutes.

"I've told you it's a variation," I said. "Could you sum up the rest of my case against William, Mr. Bonsett?"

"He's already told you that Robert didn't die in that crash," Vernia said.

"I know. I'm just trying to sort things out."

Bonsett smiled at the ceiling while he concentrated. "It was based on Robert's ability to fly the plane, his resemblance to William, and the fact that Lynn Baxter had known both brothers. Its major virtue was explaining why the plane had been found south of Long Island. The idea of an elopement to Maryland is a clever explanation, by the way, but it's rather unsupported."

"You don't believe it's psychologically sound?" I asked.

"That a young girl could have a weakness for a draftee?" he asked. "It's sound enough for a paperback romance."

"To back it up, I have the testimony of Mildred Fell."

"The nurse who ran off with Carteret," Bonsett said.

"Who was carried off," I said. "This is the first important point. I believe Robert Carteret was trying to complete an earlier elopement when he married Mildred. She described him as being fairly lucid during their time together, but I think she's been fooling herself. Nothing he did backs up that idea. I believe he was only well enough to act out his recollections of those few days from 1941. Robert wanted Mildred to run off with him to Maryland for a quick service, but she was smart enough not to leave the city. He didn't get that idea from watching television, in my opinion. The other indication that he was re-creating a role is his unexplained return to his inner world following their short honeymoon. I think he'd simply run out of obsession."

"I don't think Mildred Fell's golden memories would convince a jury," Bonsett said.

"None of this will come before a jury," Harry said. "Isn't that right, Owen?"

"Yes and no, Harry, as always. Certainly not a jury of twelve. You three are the jury. My proofs have to satisfy you."

Bonsett became stuffy for a moment. "I won't presume to pass judgment on Robert Carteret."

Carolyn Vernia smiled for the first time, showing me that she'd understood.

So had Harry. "You're not on trial here, Owen," he said.

"Go ahead, Mr. Keane," Vernia said, "I'll hear the rest of your defence."

"Owen."

"Relax, Harry. No one will carry me off while you're around. I'm just getting to the good part anyway. Would you continue your summation, Mr. Bonsett?"

"Let me see, Robert and the girl decided to elope to Maryland. I suppose the plane suggested itself for speed."

"And because it was prepped for the Albany flight. Robert had flown it back to the estate the day before."

"You learned that from the mechanic?" Bonsett asked.

"Yes, Gustave Warden."

"He told you the plane had been tampered with?"

"He told me that simple carelessness couldn't account for the oil loss that caused the crash. He suggested that the oil had been deliberately contaminated with water, which turned to steam as the engine heated up. Over New Jersey the pressure blew the oil cap into orbit—it wasn't found with the wreckage—and most of the oil went with it."

"From which informed judgment you moved to the conclusion that William had sabotaged the plane, perhaps after hearing of the elopement plans while hiding behind a potted plant." Bonsett was getting into the spirit of the proceedings.

"Something like that," I said.

"Why didn't he shoot them, Mr. Keane?" Bonsett asked. "Sabotaging an airplane is an awkward way to murder someone."

"Important point number two. Suppose you weren't thinking of murder. Suppose you considered yourself the injured party, and you were simply seeking justice. Contaminating the oil might make sense to you. If they didn't run off with the plane, if they changed their minds, or if you'd simply been mistaken, they wouldn't be hurt."

Carolyn Vernia was true to her corporate forefathers. "I still don't believe William was capable of it," she said.

"In his defense, I think he had a change of heart." I said. "I have it on good authority that he broke up a scheduled meeting that morning and rushed back to the estate. He didn't make it in time, of course."

"You haven't spoken with any of the servants, have you?" Bonsett asked.

"As I told Miss Vernia, I don't even know if any are still alive. Her father closed the place down during the war. The only one kept on was a grounds keeper named Gregson. We'll get to him later.

"Now we'll break new ground. The first mystery I solved was the nine-month disappearance of the *Phaeton*. I should have guessed it sooner, but my geography is weak. The plane crashed in the New Jersey Pine Barrens. It's a pretty interesting region, believe it or not. Miles of pine trees and sand, with a few ghost towns thrown in. For our purposes, although, it's crossed by paved roads, it could easily have hidden the wreck of a small plane."

"We can congratulate you on that much," Harry said. Neither Vernia nor Bonsett joined in. It was a tough day for the home team.

"I visited the Pine Barrens yesterday," I continued. "To be precise, I was standing on the site of the crash at five o'clock yesterday evening, give or take a few minutes. It took me every minute of five hours to get back to the city. As the crow flies it's only a hundred miles or so, but for a man on foot the journey is rather involved. To begin with, I had to find my way out of the forest. My guide had quit without notice. But I'm getting ahead of myself. We'll call the five-hour trip point three and get back to it.

"I went down there to check the local sheriff's office for records of the crash investigation. Unfortunately, the records had been lost in a fire. I then went to the county newspaper, where I posed as a free-lance journalist." Carolyn Vernia colored at the mention of the newspaper. I paused for a comment, but she held her peace. "I examined the local newspaper coverage of the crash and learned that there was a significant difference in the injuries suffered by the two victims. They both died of head injuries, as near as anyone could tell after nine months. But Lynn Baxter's skull was cracked, while Carteret's was crushed. Point number four.

"The difference becomes more interesting when you consider the crash itself. Robert never lost full control of the plane, according to Gus Warden, even though he couldn't check the descent. In fact, he almost made it to a paved road, Highway Five Thirty-nine. He probably could have landed the plane safely if the ground hadn't been wooded. As it was, he did a remarkable job. Photographs of the crash site show that the plane's fuselage was almost intact.

"The newspaper editor I spoke with suggested that I visit a local historian who lives off Five Thirty-nine near the crash site. His name is James Skiles. Historian may be too dignified a title for Skiles. He's really a storyteller. He's the one who stranded me in the woods. Before our relationship broke down, he told me a story that made the whole trip worthwhile. It seems that the ghost of William Carteret still walks in that part of the Pines."

I paused to take stock of my audience. Bonsett seemed to be too busy memorizing my speech to react. Vernia was leaning forward slightly, holding my rose in folded hands. Harry was finally paying more attention to me than to our guests.

"He walks in his aviator's costume, complete with scarf and leather jacket. His hands and face are covered with blood, and he cries as he walks."

"Did you see him?" Bonsett asked.

"No. I didn't hear him either. Most people just hear him."

"Are we supposed to believe any of this?" Vernia might have been asking permission.

"Part of it. The first sighting, which is the basis of the whole legend, was made by a local woman named Ann, in broad daylight. Ann saw a bloody pilot fighting his way through the forest. Almost scared the life out of her. She eventually got around to telling the locals her tale, but no one took her seriously enough to go back and look for a plane. When the wreck was finally found, the clothes on the pilot matched Ann's description pretty closely. It was also obvious from the condition of his head that the man hadn't walked a foot since he'd crashed. Not alive anyway. Hence the ghost story. That's the last point, by the way, point five."

Bonsett was still looking for holes. "Couldn't this Ann have stumbled on the actual wreck and made up the story of the crying man?"

"That's a possible explanation," I admitted, "but I think it requires an unnecessary leap."

Carolyn Vernia let out a flat laugh. "Certainly it's less of a leap to believe in ghosts," she said.

Something in her nervousness calmed me. I needed calming at that moment. "I don't believe in ghosts," I said. "I believe Ann saw a man walk away from the wreck. The blood on his hands and face belonged to the dead girl. He wasn't hurt badly himself. And he wasn't William Carteret."

Vernia the paperback mystery veteran was way ahead of the other two. "You walked out of the forset yesterday," she said. "You made it to New York City in five hours."

"Yes," I said. "First walking, then hitchhiking, then taking a cab and a train. I took advantage of my opportunities, just as Robert Carteret did in 1941."

Bonsett started to speak, but his boss cut him off. "You're not thinking," she said. "Robert would have hired a car."

"Possibly," I said. "Robert had a couple of other advantages over me. He started earlier in the day, maybe as early as twelve-thirty or one o'clock. The day was clear, so he had the sun to guide him out of the forest. And they tell me that before the Parkway came along, Highway Five Thirty-nine had been a pretty busy road.

"I give Robert an hour of wandering in shock after the crash. Ann saw him sometime during that period. Then he recovered somewhat."

"He decided that William had caused the crash," Vernia said.

"Yes. Ann described him as swinging and tearing at the forest as he went. I think he directed that same emotion toward his brother. Robert had been forced to a primitive spot, both literally and emotionally, by the actions of his brother and the death of Lynn Baxter. Now he dragged WIlliam in after him. He found him at the estate on Long Island. I've been told that Robert had the stronger character of the two. I don't doubt that he dominated William that night. He forced his brother back to find the wreck of the plane. They traveled a great distance in a drive of a few hours. They traveled too far from their home and their privilege and their normal lives to ever come back. Neither one did really. One of them was certainly crazy during that drive, and fear and remorse probably turned the other. If not, maybe the place did, the forest. It was incredible that the setting could exist so close to these two and their empty, easy world. Incredible and perfect, because the setting matched what they'd become so well it made what happened next almost natural. I felt that yesterday in the forest before I understood it, felt the insignificance of the order we four live by, its lack of depth and reach.

"Robert showed William the body of the dead girl. And then Robert killed him."

I'd been playing to Carolyn Vernia during my speech, and I hadn't noticed that Bonsett had risen from his chair. "And what did William do? Stand there like a sheep?"

The office had the stillness of a stage. I read my next lines slowly. "We have Robert's own testimony on that, oddly enough. Mildred Fell told me something that confused me at first. After the war, Carteret would have bad periods, 'bad nights,' she called them. Sometimes he'd call out for Lynn Baxter. Sometimes he would protect his head with his arms, against some attack that only he could see. He'd yell..."

"No, Robert, no," Carolyn Vernia said calmly. Her large brown eyes were staring past me through the office window. "He still yells it," she said.

TWENTY-SEVEN

BONSETT WAS STANDING at one of Harry's windows, watching the morning traffic. Carolyn Vernia was still in her seat, and she was still staring toward the window behind me. I couldn't guess what she was watching. Harry looked embarrassed. He offered me a cigarette, thought better of it, and lit one himself. His fingers played nervously on the desktop. It would be a hard night for the neighbors, I thought, when Harry got home to his clarinet.

At the moment, we weren't going anywhere. Our intermission had stretched to ten minutes. Already that morning I'd reached a point beyond the experience of most movie detectives. I had announced a farfetched theory with no dramatic result. No one had cracked. No killer, crazed with guilt, had sprung at me to provide the needed proof. None could, of course, but it was awkward all the same. I'd reached the end of my plan.

Finally, Bonsett turned to face us. He'd apparently been organizing his attack in his minutes by the window. He ignored his chair on the walk back and stood, with legs spread apart, in front of Harry's desk. He was too short for the stance to be intimidating, but it conveyed some legal signal to Harry, who sat up and ground out his cigarette.

"Would you like to hear my objections to your theory in any particular order?" Bonsett asked. I didn't answer. "I'll give them in the order of greatest non-sense, then."

I was more interested in my reaction to Bonsett than I was in his speech. I wasn't worried or embarrassed or angry. I'd defended or tried to defend my opinion on a hundred more important subjects without the conviction I felt now. The morning was going better than I'd hoped. For the moment at least, I felt a peace of mind I hadn't known for some time. It should have made Robert Carteret and Owen Keane even, but I wanted more.

"And then there's the business of finding the plane," Bonsett was saying. "You can't have Robert and William arriving at the forest before sunset. How could they possibly have found the plane in the dark?"

Bonsett sounded like an editor poking holes in a plot summary I'd submitted. Even that didn't bother me. "I don't know," I said. "They might not have found the plane until the next morning. It doesn't matter. I know they searched until they found it. I know that because William's body was found there nine months later. The idea of the two of them stumbling around in the dark all night doesn't make the picture any prettier."

"What picture?" Bonsett was losing his professional patience. "I've already told you that your evidence is circumstantial where it isn't actually fantastic. What are even more damning are the gaps in the evidence you have. From the time William Carteret broke up his meeting on October 10, 1941, until Robert reported for duty five days later, you don't have a single witness. Except, of course, for a woman with no last name who saw a ghost in the woods."

"Ann was her last name," I said. "Her first name was Blueberry."

"Owen," Harry said.

"Can you produce her?" Bonsett asked.

"Dead," I said.

"Hearsay, then. You seem to think if a thing is psychologically or physically possible it is automatically true. You don't even have a witness for the Baxter girl's change of heart, one of the bases of your theory. You haven't tried to explain why Robert Carteret was never recalled from the service, why no murder investigation ever took place. If they had the evidence of tampering you suggest, why didn't they follow it up?"

"That particular part of the story didn't tax my imagination," I said. "The records of the government crash investigators are on file in this city, available for anyone to see. It's hard to explain why no one continued the investigation. I'm afraid, Miss Vernia, that I need to bring your father in if I'm even to make a try at it.

"The absence of witnesses and evidence is the result of coincidence or the passage of time or something else. I know it's the weakness of our age to think in terms of conspiracies, but the secrecy that was built up around Robert's disability supports the idea of an earlier cover-up. Suggests a continuing motive anyway.

"In my scheme of things, Robert didn't have time to cover his tracks. Neither did William for that matter. I don't think Robert had the heart, either. He didn't switch clothes with his brother and enter the army to escape the law. He'd already become his own law, and I think he'd already decided to die. Unfortunately, sentence was passed by a tougher judge at Anzio.

"Something or someone protected Robert before and after he was wounded. I don't think we have to look further than the man who replaced his brother as president of Carteret Federal Bank." That brought Carolyn Vernia back to us, but not to object. Her expression told me that I was reaching the meat of my discussion as far as she was concerned.

Bonsett was the one who objected. "This is what I meant when I said your evidence is fantastic. You're taking a great leap from the simple act of closing the house on Long Island. Surely that was normal enough in wartime."

"Normal enough. Dismissing the staff was normal enough. Keeping one man on, a grounds keeper, to watch over the place was normal enough. The caretaker's name was Peter Gregson. I mentioned him earlier. Gregson starts out normal enough himself, but his role grows and grows. In 1941, he was just a name in the crash report, the last man to see the Carteret plane. Mildred Fell remembers him from the early fifties as a garrulous old man. Ten years later he was an abusive drunk, lording some mysterious power over everyone on the estate, even Carteret."

"What power?" Bonsett asked.

"The ability to get away with things, to hang on when everyone else was let go, to be paid for work he didn't do, to drink himself to death free of charge. Blackmail can't help but grow like that. It feeds on its success.

"Gregson slept in the carriage house loft, the second floor of the Carteret garage. There was a hole in his floor, a knothole. Toward the end of his life, Gregson would call it a magic hole. He'd joke that all the whiskey he drank came from that hole."

"How could you know that?" Vernia asked. I'd finally succeeded in impressing her.

I tapped the side of my head. "Omniscience," I said. "Gregson would also claim that you could hear the voice of the dead through that hole. He'd done it himself, on the night we've been talking about. I don't think Robert Carteret hired a car that night, Miss Vernia. Gregson heard them together in the garage below his room. It wasn't valuable right away. It was nine months before anyone was sure William was dead. After that, Gregson had a meal ticket for life."

"Why would Carl Vernia allow himself to be blackmailed?" Bonsett asked. "He'd done nothing wrong himself."

"For the same reason he kept Robert's illenss a secret, whatever that was. He couldn't laugh off an investigation that would show the world the real Robert Carteret."

Bonsett pressed his point. "Why would he hide Carteret's condition? What was his motive?"

"Not 'Why would he?' Mr. Bonsett. Why did he? As I see it, there's a range of possibilities. He might have wanted to build a corporation from someone else's bank. Or he might have felt he owed the Carterets. He might have spent his life protecting Robert out of loyalty to Charles Carteret, Robert's father. I don't know. No one I talked with knew Carl Vernia well enough to venture a guess."

"No one knew him that well," his daughter said slowly. "I'd be surprised if he understood his own motives."

During the short silence that followed, Bonsett returned to his seat. Carolyn Vernia studied Ms. Kiefner's rose.

"You're right, Miss Vernia," I said after a time. "I'm sorry if I make it all sound cut and dried. It's an occupational hazard."

"Your occupation is fraught with hazards at the moment," she replied. Her phrasing suggested that she'd divided her reading time between mysteries and romances. "I require a promise of more than discretion from you and your firm, Mr. Keane," she continued.

I expected Harry to issue the standard disclaimer, but he sat there, looking at me blankly. It was a bad time for him to revert to the Watson role.

"As a member of this firm," I said, "you can rely on my keeping my mouth shut. However, that warranty is only good until noon or so. I should have my desk cleaned out by then. I've decided that I can't work for Mr. Ohlman anymore."

"I'm in the room, Owen," Harry said. "You can address me."

"Sorry, Harry. I'm resigning because you violated a confidence that is more important to me than the crash of the *Phaeton* is to any of us."

"If you're referring to the small insight into your past Mr. Ohlman gave us, I think you're overreacting," Vernia said.

"Nevertheless, I've made up my mind."

"What's going on here?" Bonsett demanded. "What are you trying to set up?"

"Nothing," I said.

Bonsett pressed me. "Are you trying to exempt your firm from responsibility?"

"Just a personal career decision."

"Career decision? You're not after a job, are you?"

"Something like Peter Gregson's old position?" I asked. "No, I'm not interested in early retirement."

"You do want something, though, don't you?" Vernia asked.

"Yes," I said.

Bonsett almost stood up again. "I believe Miss Vernia discussed our attitude toward blackmail with you on an earlier occasion."

"Scared me to death."

"What do you want, Mr. Keane?" Vernia asked.

"I want to see Robert Carteret. I tried last week and didn't get very far. It's the only loose string in the business."

"An incredible statement coming from you," Bonsett said.

"Do you expect a confession?" Vernia asked. "If you do, you're a fool. He can't remember what he did yesterday."

"Then he can't tell me anything I shouldn't know. There aren't any bad guys left, as far as I'm concerned. There's only one victim, Robert Carteret. If you can assure me that he's being decently treated, I'll forget the entire matter. But I've got to be sure."

"You have our word," Bonsett said.

"No offence, Mr. Bonsett, but lawyer and liar are the same word in some languages. I want to see for myself."

There was an uncomfortable moment or two of silence. I felt exposed, now that I'd separated myself from Harry. I'd underestimated how much I depended on his unwilling support. I tried to catch his eye, but he was studying the dark reflections in his desktop. He looked up when Carolyn Vernia spoke.

"I almost wish this were a book or a movie," she said addressing me. "The only reasonable course of action I can think of is to have our driver run you over with the car as you leave." She sighed. "If you wish to see Robert Carteret, Lawrence will arrange it."

Bonsett covered his surprise quickly. "Of course we will insist that you sign..."

"Nothing," Vernia cut in. "I insist that you visit Mr. Carteret in your professional capacity as a member of this firm and that Mr. Ohlman accompany you. Do you agree, Mr. Ohlman?"

"Yes," Harry said.

"Mr. Keane?"

"Yes."

"Good. You know where the estate is located, I believe. Be there at two o'clock this afternoon. Satisfy yourself that Carteret is receiving the best of care. Submit a bill for your services. And never contact me or anyone else regarding the matter again." She stood up, laying the rose on Harry's desk. Her businesslike tone gave way to a wearier, quieter one. "When Donald Schiel first revived the legend, I thought it would be interesting, believe it or not. Maybe it's our current fascination with genealogy. Maybe I think of them all as family somehow. I even enjoyed your early efforts, Mr. Keane. But this story of yours has made me sad.''

"I'm sorry," I said.

"The fault is mine for underestimating you," she replied. She made me a present of a sad smile. "I didn't think you would succeed, but I suspect that you surprised even yourself, which consoles me somewhat for my poor judgment.

"Good day, gentlemen."

TWENTY-EIGHT

IT WAS RAINING as we left the city, but there were patches of blue between the clouds by the time we reached Long Island. Harry drove aggressively, changing lanes frequently and banging his horn like a cab driver. He didn't speak. His silence didn't bother me at first—the alternatives I could imagine weren't appealing—but I weakened as we neared Great Bay. The small success I was hoping to consolidate had to include a peace with Harry. Another truce, anyway.

"Nice car," I said. "Tommy takes special care of you."

"This is my car," Harry said, "as you very well know."

"I should have guessed by the way you're caressing the horn. That was a joke, by the way."

"Sorry," Harry said, without sounding it.

"Have you ever noticed that our friendship consists of a series of injuries?" I asked. "One of us is always offended."

"I've noticed that time has done nothing to improve our relationship, or my understanding of it," Harry replied.

I noted the demotion, but let it pass. "Meeting me was unkind fate, Harry. You're the type of person who would talk a stranger off a ledge, and you've always seen me as someone with one foot in the air."

"Both feet this time. I can't believe you talked your way out of that mess with that story you dreamed up. You should be selling something."

"Thanks. Maybe I'll take that up."

"As sharp as she is, Carolyn Vernia never did figure out why you want to see Carteret. Even when you were laying on the malarkey about how noble her father might have been, giving her a way out of hating him, she didn't see it."

"But you did," I said.

"Because I know you, Owen," Harry said. "You'll always be more confessor than detective. You're more interested in absolutions than solutions. You're so damn compulsive about forgiving sins, I can't believe you didn't make it as a priest."

A stray drop of water fell from an overpass and landed on our windshield. I watched as the wind moved it sideways across the glass. "There were other requirements," I said.

Harry drove another mile or so without sounding his horn. "I'm sorry," he said. "That last crack was out of line."

"Already forgiven," I said. "Compulsively."

"Did you resign to punish me or to protect the firm or to put an edge on your threat to blow the lid on Carteret?"

"Yes," I said.

"I didn't sell you out with Carolyn Vernia, Owen," Harry said. "I wanted her to understand you, so she wouldn't see you as a threat. If I spoke too freely, it was an error in judgment."

"I understand."

"If you really do, you're being unreasonable. There's no need for you to quit your job."

"Except that it's not a job as much as an Ohlman charity."

"Don't kid yourself. I might talk a stranger off a ledge, but I wouldn't pay him for the privilege. You've always carried your weight with us. And you've done more with this business than I ever expected."

"Or wanted, which is the point. It's not that I can't produce a product. There's just no market for it. Besides, you've had custody of me long enough. You've got your own child to raise."

The green front gates of the Carteret estate were open. We drove through them without talking to the guard on the intercom. I couldn't help feeling the irony of the pine trees that protected the house from the road. Beyond them, the grounds were simple but well kept. Gregson would have been pleased. The asphalt drive turned to gravel thirty yards from the formal-looking brick house. There were two large cars parked in the curve of the drive that passed by the front door.

That door opened quickly to our knock. Dr. Donald Schiel stood on the other side. "Surprise," Schiel said. "It's good to see you again, Owen." He introduced himself to Harry. "Bonsett's in the kitchen looking for a libation. It's down the hall there if either of you is interested."

Harry nodded and left us. We were standing in a large entryway that was furnished with a single grouping of chair, table, and mirror, and painted white. A stairway to our right rose to a landing that formed a false ceiling across the front of the room. Schiel studied the ceiling for a moment and assumed his odd half-smile. I prepared myself to receive another apology.

"I'm glad you turned out to be a better detective than I was a client," Schiel said. "I suppose you know I called Carolyn Vernia the evening I spoke with you. It wasn't that I doubted you, Owen, exactly. I simply couldn't see Carolyn as the villain. And I couldn't take a chance of her becoming another victim."

"I think you did the right thing," I said.

"You do? Well, I suppose I had statistical probability on my side. Speaking of which, what would you say the odds are of your solution being correct?"

"Fifty-fifty."

"You've put a lot on an even-money bet."

All I had, I reflected, but that wasn't much. "Is Carteret up to an interview?"

Schiel shrugged. "He might enjoy the company, but I wouldn't expect too much. I hope you're not planning something drastic. I don't want him shocked, whatever the motive. I'm serious now, okay?"

"Okay."

"Bonsett wanted to have you frisked for a photograph of Lynn Baxter or a model airplane or something equally sinister. I don't think he likes you."

"Just doing my job, Doctor." Bonsett had come up to us quietly. Harry trailed a few steps behind him. "Are we still waiting for that Pritchard woman?" Bonsett asked.

"Carteret's secretary?"

"His nurse, Mr. Keane," Bonsett said. "Another strand for your web. Here she is, at last."

The nurse was a thin woman nearing sixty, with elaborately piled gray hair. She didn't smile at any of us, and her curt nods during Bonsett's introductions suggested reservations. She expressed them after a pointed silence. "Mr. Carteret is having a calm day today, gentlemen. Our last few weeks haven't been this quiet."

"We won't be here long," Schiel assured her. "We're as interested in the facilities as anything else. Let's start with the nickel tour."

She nodded and led us back toward the kitchen. It was a large room with a wall of small-paned windows that must have made it a cheerful place years ago. Now tall trees blocked them, and the woman who turned as we entered was working under fluorescent light.

"This is Anna, our full-time dietitian," Pritchard said.

"What other staff do you have?" Harry asked.

"Besides Anna and myself, we have a housekeeper and her assistant, a night nurse, and two caretakers."

"Caretakers?" I repeated.

"Guards," Bonsett said.

"Who maintains the grounds?" I asked, thinking again of the infamous Gregson.

"You're not here to observe the condition of the grass, Mr. Keane." Bonsett evidently hadn't found his drink.

"A local landscaping firm," the nurse said. She led us from the kitchen through another door. "We have a television room with a small library on this floor for the staff. Except for the caretakers' rooms, the rest of the floor has been closed. My room and those of the household staff are on the second floor. Our night nurse commutes. Will you want to see any of the staff quarters?"

"That won't be necessary," Bonsett said. He gave me a quick look for confirmation.

As we ascended the broad stairway, Nurse Pritchard droned on. She and Harry led the way, followed by Bonsett and me. Dr. Schiel stayed a step or two behind us.

"Mr. Carteret's suite is on the second floor. There is also an exercise room. Generally, though, Mr. Carteret takes his exercise out of doors." We paused on the landing before a circular window that overlooked the front lawn. "Of the original sixty acres, we have eleven left. Mr. Carteret takes three walks a day, weather permitting, generally on a trail through the pine forest to the west of the house."

Bonsett's reaction to that innocent item must have renewed Ms. Pritchard's reservations. He shot me a quick accusing glance.

"Circumstantial," I said.

At the doorway to Carteret's room, the nurse stopped us again. "There are really too many of you for one visit," she said. "Please speak one at a time. Try not to move around too much once you've situated yourselves inside the room."

Bonsett waved Harry and me ahead without speaking. The room we entered was large and a cheerful yellow, but there was the same absence of pictures and personal items that characterized the rest of the house. The floor was tiled in a dated black-and-white pattern. There was a large area rug in the center of the room. On the rug were two chairs, a rocker and an armchair, and a television set. There was some sort of needlepoint project resting on the seat of the rocker. A gray-haired man sat in the armchair. Isolated in the center of the room, the little grouping looked like a museum exhibit: Retirement, circa 1981.

Robert Carteret turned in his seat as we crossed the linoleum, then stood up to face us. He was too old to be the romantic figure of my story, too thin and too short. His gray hair was close cut, but I couldn't see a mark or depression to indicate an old wound. He wore a bright green golf shirt and loud plaid slacks, which disturbed me somehow more than his age. His face was surprisingly lined for a man who had sat out the last few decades. The eyes behind his glasses were blue and distrustful. The distrust increased as he looked at each of us in turn.

Nurse Pritchard began a vague explanation of our visit that involved the bank and contained frequent references to another explanation given earlier that afternoon and already forgotten, Robert listened with the same unchallenging, unbelieving expression.

"Sit down, Robert," Schiel said.

"Been sitting all day," Carteret replied.

"I'm Dr. Schiel. You remember me."

"Of course," Robert said.

Schiel didn't believe him. He started in on a series of small reminiscences intended to establish him as an old acquaintance. While Schiel talked, I studied Carteret.

My feelings as I watched him reminded me of Carolyn Vernia's response to my solution. I wondered again why it had saddened her. Had the story she'd grown up with been any less sad? Two young people die in an accident and another is hopelessly wounded. What had made my story sadder than that? Not just that in the end they had brought it on themselves, I decided. It was sadder because a romantic passion had failed to save any of them, to justify their lives, to ennoble this lined, wasted man. That made my version sadder for me at least.

Schiel was running out of small talk. He looked at me. "Any questions, Owen?"

Robert followed Schiel's glance. He studied me, trying to place me in his empty catalog, and I recognized the process that, repeated over and over, had worn his face. After a second or two he gave up. "Haven't we met before?" he asked.

The correct answer seemed silly after the events of the last few days. "No," I said. "Is there..." What? Anything you need? Anything you want to tell me? Anything? I already knew the answer to every question I could think of. It was always the same answer, what Marilyn had called "a knock on the head."

"Excuse me?" Robert prompted.

Harry's remarks from our drive came back to me now. He'd been unusually insightful. I did want to absolve Carteret of something he didn't know to confess. Something he didn't even remember until the sunny days ran out and left him with a bad night. It required assigning him a sin that predated his moment-to-moment existence. A sin to justify the inequity and absurdity of it. Old problems blended with new ones for me. I gave up without a fight.

"Is there anything good on television?" I asked.

Robert turned to check. His face was less troubled momentarily. "Silly show," he said. "About a garbage collector and his son. He's pretending to have a heart attack. I like it, though. It's funny."

I agreed and waited for the nurse to begin our goodbyes. Instead, Carteret took a step closer to me. He began questioning me with the embarrassing license of a relative.

"Married, young man?" he asked.

"No," I said.

"No or not yet?"

"I don't know."

"What do you do for a living?"

That question caught me up, unnecessarily. I could have said anything from astronaut to zoologist. Dr. Schiel stepped into the gap. "He's a researcher, Robert."

"Researcher of what?" Carteret asked.

I could almost hear Schiel's eyes twinkling as he answered. "Mysteries. He traces lost souls. Unlocks dark secrets."

Bonsett moved from my left around behind me toward Schiel. To shut him up, I hoped.

Carteret looked at me with more interest. "Is that so?" he asked.

"Not exactly," I said. My inability to help Carteret had deflated me somehow. The emotional high ground I'd recently found seemed to be melting away beneath me, leaving me dangling above the old void. "I solve little mysteries," I said. "I haven't had much luck with the big ones."

"But you keep at it," Carteret said, nodding his gray head encouragingly.

"Yes," I said. "I keep at it."

"Why?" he demanded, his eyes suddenly narrowing behind his glasses.

His change of tack took me by surprise, and I stopped to think. "It's my job," I finally said. "It's the only thing I want to do."

Carteret beamed his approval at me. "That's right," he said. "That's exactly right, young man." He reached out and put his hand on my shoulder. "You keep at it," he said.

I stood silently, watching the worn face as it smiled its happy blessing upon me. It occurred to me that my client had paid me for my services in full.

Nurse Pritchard stepped forward. "Thank you for coming to see us, gentlemen," she said to the group.

"Thank you," Robert said to me.

TWENTY-NINE

I WAS THE QUIET ONE during the drive back. I watched the sun's reflection in the wet fields we passed and considered Carteret's unexpected affirmation. He'd turned the tables on me, forgiving me for my inability to somehow make his damaged life right. I knew, though, that I'd really turned the tables on myself, as always, that I'd tried to turn my rare moment of triumph into my standard acknowledgment of defeat. Carteret had saved me. Unknowingly, he'd set my foot back on the path. It was worthwhile to keep trying, to keep searching. I had the word of a fragmented, haunted man for that, a man who had already forgotten that I existed. Well, I took my support where I found it.

Harry's third attempt at conversation got through to me. "You've never told me about this Marilyn," he said.

"She's a friend of mine," I replied, wondering as I said it if that were still true. "You'd like her, Harry. She's got both feet on the ground and her eyes wide open."

It was Harry's day for deft insights. "Doesn't sound like your type," he said.

"That's her opinion, too," I said.

I watched the road ahead for a time. It was smooth new asphalt with still-white lines, and it wound now through small hills that seemed as dense with foliage as any rain forest. It was a prospect to hold your interest, every turn bringing some new thing.

"Now what?" Harry asked.

What indeed, I thought. There were enough stray particulars to keep me busy for a day or two. I had to clean out my desk at Ohlman, Ohlman, and Pulsifer and kiss Ms. Kiefner good-bye. I had to return Lois Parnell's photographs and repay her for their use with some safe fragment of truth. I had to trek back into the Pines to rescue my long-suffering car and to hear Jim Skiles's secret. I had to visit Mary and meet her new baby. I might even give Marilyn another chance to ask me to keep in touch. And then what?

I took my support where I found it and my guidance as well. Perhaps, after all, Carteret's empty head was a receiver for the subtle whispers of the universe, like a seashell through which you hear a phantom ocean.

"I keep at it," I said.

FIRST WIFE, TWICE REMOVED
CLARE CURZON

A THAMES VALLEY MYSTERY

First Time in Paperback

TOXIC LOVE

Two disturbing deaths have Superintendent
Mike Yeadings's team spread out from the Thames
Valley to Amsterdam, looking for answers.

The first victim, Penny Winter, a divorced mother
of two, dies as a result of food poisoning. Someone
sent her tainted pâté with intent to kill. The
second victim, Anneke Vroom, was a young Dutch
national found crammed into an antique mahogany
chest. She was shot full of heroin—and pregnant.

As the investigation of the separate incidents
develops in sinister parallel, the men and women
of the Thames Valley Police Force will confront
more untimely deaths before tangled skeins come
together to create a diabolical tapestry of murder.

"Clever misdirection."   —*Kirkus Reviews*

Available in May at your favorite retail stores.

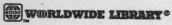

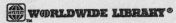

DEATH by DEGREES
Eric Wright

First Time in Paperback

An Inspector Charlie Salter Mystery

LITERALLY—AND FIGURATIVELY—DEAD

The politics and infighting to elect a new dean at Toronto's Bathurst College turns to murder when the winner is discovered dead.

Though the case appears open-and-shut—an interrupted burglary and a suspect neatly arrested—Inspector Charlie Salter believes otherwise when he begins investigating anonymous notes warning that the killer lurks in the groves of academe.

Scandal, blackmail and layers of deception line the corridors at the college...all the way to the dark truth surrounding the killer's identity.

"Excellent series...humor and insight."
—*New York Times Book Review*

Available in June at your favorite retail stores.

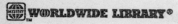
WORLDWIDE LIBRARY ®

DEGREES

This June , for the first time in paperback

NEW YORK TIMES BESTSELLING AUTHORS:

SUE GRAFTON TONY HILLERMAN

and many more...

Bring you

2ND CULPRIT

Newcomers, international names and old favorites
offer up a varied itinerary for the adventurous traveler
in crime! Join *New York Times* bestselling authors
TONY HILLERMAN and SUE GRAFTON, plus
an additional cast of 24 of the mystery genre's most
popular authors, for 2ND CULPRIT, a choice
collection of short stories.

Available in June wherever
Worldwide Mystery books are sold.

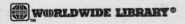

A
JOHN
COFFIN
MYSTERY

CRACKING
OPEN A
COFFIN
GWENDOLINE
BUTLER

First Time in Paperback

CONFRONTING THE ENEMY

A string of murders that had begun in the past was
working its way to the present. The victims were
young women whose lives reached from the Second
City of London's university to a refuge for battered
women—two institutions at opposite ends of the
social spectrum, yet connected by death.

Chief Commander John Coffin had seen most varieties
of evil in his career, but life had taught him there was
always scope for more. The killer in this case seems
willing to wait years for the right victim, the right mood.
He is fastidious, hard to satisfy, but get them right and
he does his job with pleasure.

The complex web of interlocking cases opens a
Pandora's box in Coffin's professional and personal
life. Too many secrets, too much twisted emotion, too
much treachery among friends...one of whom may be
a killer.

"An awesome plot.... Truly terrific."   —*MLB News*

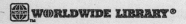

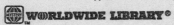